midnight and mercy

Midnight AND Mercy

by

Tracy Broemmer

Contemporary Romance

Published by Tracy Broemmer

Edited by Lexie Broemmer

Cover by Vanilla Lily Designs

ISBN#: 978-1-965331-16-3

one

. . .

WY

Divorce didn't necessarily mean free. And gone didn't necessarily mean safe.

Wynona Herzog flicked her eyes to the rearview mirror and watched the empty road behind her a moment too long. Beside her, in the passenger seat, fifteen-year-old Declan scoffed at her—not even bothering to hide it with a cough. She didn't have to look at him to know he rolled his eyes. Her son was a gifted eye-roller. Had been for some time.

Unfortunately, she and Zach were at fault.

Probably, with the eight hundred plus miles between her little Honda SUV and Sioux Falls, South Dakota, the only thing chasing her anymore was ghosts. But damned if ghosts weren't scarier, possibly deadlier, than exes.

Shoulders frozen like stone, Wy eased her white-knuckle grip on the steering wheel and glanced at Dec. AirPods tucked in his ears, he sat back in his seat with his head turned to the passenger window. His unruly hair curled around his ears, down over the crewneck collar of his Metallica t-shirt. He needed a haircut, but her son's hair was the least of her concerns right now. She had learned long ago to choose her battles, and short of bright green or a mohawk, she wouldn't ride Declan's ass about it.

His hands rested in his lap; no seatbelt crossed over his waist. Since becoming a teen, Declan had dipped his hands into bad behavior. He was experimenting, seeing what acts of defiance he could get away with. Pushing Wy further and further, leaving her feeling helpless and hopeless.

Which was nothing new.

Except that now her worry about Declan was her sole focus.

The phone call earlier this afternoon from the principal at Nelson County High was the third already this semester. Wy knew there had been warnings, so it wasn't simply the third incident—just the third since Declan had burned through said warnings.

Insolence. No surprise. Hell, wasn't most of the teen population in today's world insolent? Mean? Hateful? Yep. Add in Dec's father's DNA and the first fifteen years of his life lived under Zach's care and influence, and Wy had her hands full.

As much as she hated a smartass personality—her ex-husband was the prince of derision, contempt—it was better than the physical stuff Dec was flirting with now. She had a suspicion his warnings from both his homeroom teacher and his English teacher were related to his sharp, hateful mouth. The first two phone calls had been about vandalism. Spray painting the southern wall of the gymnasium. How in the hell Dec got a hold of spray paint in the middle of nowhere, Kentucky was beyond her. How he managed to find himself alone outside the gym on a Tuesday night an even bigger mystery. That he had painted the words *FUCK NHS* didn't blow her mind.

Nope. The word fuck was a regular part of Dec's vocabulary. She was mortified, yes. Surprised? No.

The second call had been the time he was found messing with Eileen Conner's car. He claimed he'd seen someone steal something from the front passenger seat, and he was trying to catch them. When he couldn't do that, he had opened the door to see if he could tell what was stolen. Wy had held her breath for days, worried that the music teacher would discover a big stash of cash was gone or that some kind of damage had been done to the car, and of course, *Declan* would be to blame. Not the supposed thief Dec was trying to catch.

Today's call had been typical of teen boys. Fighting in the halls. Only Declan had landed a blow so hard to a kid's face he had been taken to the hospital by ambulance. Never mind that Dec wore a black and blue necklace that looked suspiciously like a hand imprint. *Declan* had been suspended. Nothing happened to the other kid. *After all, Mrs. Herzog*—God, how she hated to be called *Mrs. Herzog*—*Evan's in the ER having his broken nose set, isn't that punishment enough?*

She needed to talk to Declan about this latest thing. Get the truth out of him. That much shouldn't be hard. Her kid was brutally honest. Tight-lipped about most things, but if and when he spoke, Wy knew he was telling the truth.

The loud wailing of a horn as a car flew by her on the old two-lane road pulled her out of her thoughts. That same sound of disdain from the passenger seat told her Declan noticed how she tensed at the noise. Sometimes, she would swear Dec made as much noise as he could, just to startle her. To see her flinch.

She hated that her son could be so cruel. Because every now and then, he wasn't. He was simply a boy whose parents had divorced. A lost boy looking for love. A boy whose father had taught him violence instead of patience.

A tremor racked her body as she considered that. Not entirely true.

She and Zach both had a hand in Declan's upbringing. And maybe somewhere deep inside, Zach loved their son. Because Wy did; she loved Declan to the moon and back. But in the end, she had been just as guilty as Zach for teaching the kid to choose violence and hatred.

two

. . .

PIERCE

The sounds of Kenny Chesney and P!nk's voices poured from the jukebox in the Iron Stag. Pierce Rooney liked country music, but he wasn't a purist, and he liked the combination. He liked Chris Stapleton's duets with the likes of Justin Timberlake and Ed Sheeran, too. He and his buddies argued that one until they were blue in the face one night; he and Cole Lockland had argued for the new blood in country. Rye Gallaher and Mav Pressey had argued for the old, classic stuff.

Pierce tipped his pint glass and studied the last swallow of beer. Warm. Probably mostly backwash. The thought turned his stomach, so he pushed the glass away and shook his head when Marlowe reached for it.

"I'm good."

"Pussy." She flashed him a wide grin. Pierce considered flipping her off, but he only laughed. He wasn't up for the verbal sparring tonight. After a full day at Lockland, he'd been called out to take care of a bonfire that got out of hand and burned a fourth of Old Man Turner's woods. His eyes were gritty with smoke and lack of sleep, and his joints ached like he had gone a round or two in the ring with an MMA fighter.

"Working tomorrow?" she asked him as she took his glass and set it in the sink behind the bar.

"You know it."

"No rest for the wicked."

"How's Way?" he asked his friend.

Rodey, Kentucky was small enough that he knew everyone who lived there. He and Marlowe had been good friends since their school days, despite a small age difference. Marlowe's son Waylon would be at home right now with her dad, who had lived with her since her mom died.

"He's good." Her smile took on the soft edges the same way all moms' smiles seemed to when they talked about their kids.

Then again, he supposed Taj Bailey's did that, too. And Taj wasn't just a dad, but a big burly hulk of a guy. Muscle on top of muscle—the guy was a retired champion bull rider, for fuck's sake. And if that wasn't enough, he had done a stint as a stripping Santa in the male revue in Kissing Springs, a neighboring small town.

Yet, if you mentioned Stella, Ellery, or Beckett to Taj, the man melted like a stick of butter left out on a kitchen counter on a summer day.

"Good." Pierce nodded.

"Hear about Evan Church?"

Pierce slid off the barstool, but he hesitated at Marlowe's question. Evan Church was the son of a girl he had graduated with. In fact, he and Amy had dated for a while. But she'd found Jesus when they were twenty, and after sleeping with him for six months, she decided she wanted to try and grow back her virginity. Spiritually or some bullshit thing. There had been no hard feelings; in fact, they were still good friends, despite Pierce having to forget all his biblical knowledge of her lithe little body and her hot little mouth.

"What about Evan?" He leaned into the bar now, rested his elbows on the polished wood.

"Got his face smashed at school today."

"What, now?" Pierce tipped his head with a frown.

"That new kid. Beat the shit out of him." Marlowe shrugged. "I don't know what started it, but Evan had to have his nose set. New kid got suspended."

"Jesus."

Part of him wanted to grouse and piss and moan about how the kid should be expelled. But he was a guy, and he used to be a teenage boy, and he had gone through all those bullshit fazes, too. He'd been the nerdy tween with braces and zits. He'd been the horny boy in algebra class always looking at boobs. And he'd been the cocky, smartass jock athlete who had picked a few fights and gotten his ass kicked a couple of times.

Then again, kids these days seemed so much more cruel than when he was a kid. It was personal, the way kids fought and bullied each other now.

"Amy and Tony talked to a lawyer." Marlowe was still talking.

"Who's the new kid?"

Marlowe shrugged. "Dunno. I've seen him and his mom around town, but I don't know who they are."

Pierce's phone buzzed in his back pocket. He slid the gadget out, holding his breath and hoping it wasn't another fire call. Seeing his sister's name and number on the screen was only a small relief. Lyndi was mostly a pain in his ass, and he usually dodged her calls.

He lifted the phone, screen out, to Marlowe. She lit up like a lightbulb and smiled.

"Tell her hey."

"What's up?" He nodded at Marlowe, tucked the phone between his shoulder and ear, and pulled his wallet from his pocket. When Marlowe took the twenty he dropped on the bar, he touched her hand and gestured for her to keep the change. She nodded her thanks.

"You don't have to talk," Lyndi said without a hello. "Just let me talk to you and pretend like I'm having a real conversation. Okay? Like we're having a deep conversation about Mom and Dad."

"Where are you?" Pierce froze on the way across the bar to the door.

"At the library," his little sister answered.

"Is someone bothering you?"

"Kind of, yeah." She cleared her throat.

"I'll kick his—"

"First, Pierce, I'm in Iowa, remember?" She laughed. "And second, no guys."

Deciding she wasn't in physical danger, maybe just tired of being harassed, Pierce started moving again and left the bar. The door closed, cutting off a George Strait song.

"What? There's a woman harassing you?"

"Mmm." She laughed. Pierce hesitated again. She sounded nervous, and Lyndi wasn't scared of anything. "A few, yeah."

"Can you leave?"

"Not sure."

Fuming, the conversation with Marlowe about Evan Church getting his nose bashed in fresh in his mind, Pierce yanked his truck door open and hauled himself up to the driver's seat.

"Who are they?"

"Don't know." Lyndi cleared her throat. "Five, I think."

"There are five women bothering you? In a library?"

"Girls," she answered with a laugh. Pierce closed his eyes and tried to imagine the scene. Were they armed? Hell, they didn't need to be, he knew that. People could be vicious. And girls were just as bad as men, sometimes.

"Can you get to your car?"

He tipped his head back to rest on the seat and sucked in a deep breath meant to calm himself. Instead, the air lit fire to the rage exploding in his chest. He and Lyndi were night and day different. She had left Rodey, Kentucky when she was eighteen, insisting she couldn't possibly live in such a confining, judgmental little town. Rodey was tiny, for sure, and he got where Lyndi was coming from about feeling confined, like her mental and physical growth could be stunted here. But he had never considered his hometown judgmental.

Then again, he walked a pretty straight and narrow line compared to the crazy, convoluted circles and helixes Lyndi walked.

"Mmm. Hang on."

The sound on her end of the call was muffled now, as if she had tucked her phone away from her mouth. While he waited, he started his truck. He would drive to Iowa if he had to. No, he and Lyndi weren't super close, but she was his sister. No one was allowed to fuck with her. Other than him, of course. That was his job, and his alone.

The situation would be long over by the time he arrived in Iowa. But if she said the word, Pierce would head there now.

"I think they're leaving."

He tried to picture it again. Could Lyndi see them leaving? What if they were only going out to the parking lot? What if they were waiting to jump her when she left the library?

"Stay on the phone with me," he ordered her.

"I'm at the window watching them. They're getting in a car."

"Anyone around who can walk you to your car?"

"No." She sounded sullen now, less animated and yet, more Lyndi. "I think they're gone."

"How did that get started?" he asked. Pierce put his truck in drive and eased out of his parking spot to head home.

"They came in right behind me. I think they're drunk. Tipsy, at least. Dripping gold and Chanel Number 5. I saw them laughing at my boots."

Pierce held his tongue. Lyndi was tiny—petite, slender and small-boned, she looked like a fairy. If only she had wings. She was also the least feminine girl he'd ever met; he knew the combat boots she mentioned. They probably weighed more than she did.

"Lyndi—"

"Thanks, Pierce."

The line went dead before he could say another word. Angry with her, and still worried about her, he shot off a text to command her to text him when she was home safe.

three

. . .

WY

"What's that for?" Wy eyed the duffel bag over Declan's shoulder with dread.

"Stayin' at Mason's tonight," he answered her without even looking in her direction. Stunned by his audacity to assume it was okay if he went to a friend's house after what he had done yesterday at school, Wy sucked in a deep breath and pressed her fingertips to the bags under her eyes.

"No."

"No what?" Declan glanced at her as he shoved a piece of cheese into his mouth.

"No, you're not going to Mason's house tonight," she said simply.

"Why not?"

"Declan." She rolled her eyes. "It's ten in the morning, and Mason, as well as the rest of your friends, are at school right now. Where you should be. You were suspended yesterday. Remember?"

"So?"

"So, no. You will not be going anywhere this weekend."

"I told you. Evan Church punched me first."

"I don't care." She shrugged. If Declan were small for his age, if he was bullied, she might be just a tiny bit proud of him for standing up for himself. She still didn't have the whole story, because Declan had refused to talk. But she doubted Evan bullied him, and obviously, her son wasn't small or helpless.

With an angry huff, he slung the duffel bag down and stomped off, leaving it lay in the middle of the kitchen floor. Working from home was supposed to be easier, but it meant being around Dec when he wasn't at school. And being around Dec had never been particularly easier. She had a meeting with a potential client in less than an hour. No sense in simmering over Declan's behavior right now. She nudged the bag out of the way but hesitated before leaving the room. The duffel was suspiciously lightweight. With a glance in the direction of the steps where Declan had climbed angrily up to his room, Wy squatted down and tugged the zipper of the black duffel open.

A pair of jeans. Three vape pens. A pack of cigarettes and a lighter. And a beat-up copy of a skin magazine. The last was the least of her concerns. While she didn't love the idea of her son spending alone time with dirty magazines or Internet porn, he was a boy, and he was at the age to be interested in nudity and sex. Actually, he was probably beyond the age of interest and possibly experimenting. Wy filed the thought away for a future conversation. For now, she was concerned about the vape pens and the cigarettes.

The faint buzz of her cell phone from the other room drew her attention from the bag. With a resigned sigh, she zipped the bag again, straightened, and made her way back to the spare bedroom she had set up to use as an office. Her meeting would be a Zoom meeting, not to mention that it was too early for that. Couldn't possibly be the principal's office calling since Dec was home with her today. Still, her stomach soured when she saw the unfamiliar number on her phone. She was well-acquainted with the Nelson County area code. This couldn't possibly be good news.

"Hello?" She dropped into the chair behind her desk and reminded herself to breathe.

"Wynona Herzog?"

"This is she."

"Hi, my name is Amy Church."

She knew the instant she saw the number; hearing the name was the only confirmation she needed. This was the mother of the boy Declan had hit yesterday. God only knew what she would have to say.

"Hi, Amy."

"I'm not even sure how to say this," the woman began. "I understand that you and I will never know what was said between our sons yesterday. And I get that my son threw the first punch. But Evan's nose is broken. My husband and I spent last night at the clinic in Kissing Springs. Dr. Larssen realigned his nose and packed it. He's in a splint, and he's home from school at least today."

"I'm sorry," Wynona said softly.

"You're sorry."

"I don't know what else to say, Amy. I am truly sorry, and I've talked to Declan."

Uncomfortable silence hung at the other end of the call for a moment. Finally, Amy made a sound of frustration, maybe disgust.

"Well, he's missing classes. He's missing football practices. Games." The woman cleared her throat. "I just want you to know if it happens again, my husband and I will press charges."

"It won't happen again—"

"I certainly hope not."

The call dropped, but Wy held the dead phone to her ear a moment longer. Her parents were older; Wynona was the youngest of five children. All her siblings and their families were scattered all over the country. And nine times out of ten, any attempt at conversation with her ex-husband ended in a shouting match. If she were to call Zach to discuss this latest development, all hell would break loose before she could get two words out.

She was truly alone in dealing with her son. As much as she cherished the space from her ex, Wy desperately needed help with Declan before things got too out of hand.

four

• • •

PIERCE

He twisted the cap off a bottle and downed a big gulp. Up in the scorekeeper's box in the Nelson County High School football stands, Jake Manson threw the switch and killed the Friday night lights. Pierce rested his elbows on the bed of his truck, soda bottle dangling between his thumb and index finger. Nelson County had pulled out a tight game to keep their record on the positive side, but they hadn't looked too good.

Then again, they never had been too good. Pierce had played when he was in school. Run of the mill running back on an average high school team, playing for fun. Never for the future.

Most of the parking lot had emptied out by now. Just after nine, Pierce was waiting, looking for Marlowe. Sometimes after home games, the two of them headed to Kissing Springs for pizza or a beer at the Bourbon Boot Scoot. Seemed like most of their friends had hooked up for good lately; he and Marlowe were just two of a few single people left their age.

While Pierce figured, *hoped*, he would fall for someone eventually, he knew without doubt it wouldn't be Marlowe. They were friends, nothing more.

He pulled his phone from his pocket as he waited. Lyndi had texted last night to tell him she had made it home okay, but he hadn't heard another word since then. Not exactly surprising, and yet, Pierce wanted an explanation. Why was a group of women stalking his little sister?

Pierce heard Marlowe before he saw her. Phone still in his left hand, soda in his right, he looked up and tipped his head, watching Marlowe approach his truck. Her phone pressed to her ear, she laughed as she listened to her caller.

"No way," she said with a quick shake of her head. Pierce liked that—when people were so carried away in a phone conversation that they talked with their hands or made crazy gestures, even though their listeners couldn't see them. Marlowe locked eyes with him over the bed of the truck. Pierce stared at her boldly, wondering who she was talking to. He hoped to hell she wasn't about to hook up with someone. That would leave him and Mav Pressey the last two single people in his group of friends. As well as he got along with Mav Pressey, he didn't relish the idea of having to hang out with him just to get time out of his small house and on the town. Mav would argue that he was a chick magnet, and while Pierce agreed women were drawn to the guy, he also knew once a woman got too close to Mav Pressey, she couldn't get far enough away fast enough.

Spending too much time with Mav Pressey would be dating suicide.

"See ya." Marlowe ended her call and aimed a smile at Pierce. "I'm freaking starving."

"Me, too."

“Let’s go eat.”

“Burgers?” Pierce’s favorite food was a burger from the Iron Stag.

“Hell, no. I don’t wanna spend my night off at the Stag.”

Even from across the truck bed, Pierce saw her roll her eyes. As much as he loved the burgers at the Stag, he knew Marlowe would say no. Still fun to tease her; she expected it by now.

“Black Olive?” He juggled his phone and soda so he could open his door.

“Now you’re talking,” she agreed as she climbed into the passenger seat. Pierce started the truck and adjusted the radio station as she buckled her seatbelt and aimed her key fob at her car a few spaces over. “What a game.”

“Nail biter,” he mumbled.

“Way decided he wants to play football.”

Pierce shot a look at Marlowe across the cab of the truck. Her son was small for his age; amid the farm boys out there on the football field, he would likely get his ass kicked and his head busted. So what if the NFL and other football leagues in turn were working to combat head injuries and concussions with newer helmet designs? Way’s size was more suited to being a Derby jockey.

“He could be a kicker,” Pierce suggested.

“Why can’t he just play baseball?” Marlowe mumbled. “Or run track?”

Pierce nodded. “Mm-hmm.” The kid was probably fast with how thin he was. But a lot of young boys wanted to play football. Pierce would have chosen football a hundred times over track.

"What the—?" He tapped the brakes hard enough to throw himself and Marlowe forward a bit. In front of them on the road between Rodey and Kissing Springs was a sheriff's car, lights flashing, a fire truck and ambulance, and two beaters piled together like a person might find at the demolition derby at a county fair.

"Car accident," Marlowe mumbled as Pierce slowed to a complete stop. He jammed the truck into park as he threw off his seatbelt and swung his door open. The back door of the ambulance was open, an EMT treating a young kid sitting on the end of a stretcher. Pierce nodded at the EMT as he made his way through the vehicles.

"Everybody okay?" he asked the deputy by the sheriff's car. George Stanfield looked at him with a quick nod.

"Yeah. Not a lot more than a fender bender, but it could have been a disaster."

"What happened?" Pierce shoved his hands in his pockets and leaned a bit to the side to see around George. The windshield of one car was shattered, the front wheel well and hood of the other car rippled like an accordion.

"Damned kids," George muttered. "Patrick Hoffman decided it would be fun to turn his headlights off and drive through the two-way stop here."

Pierce winced. He knew kids who had done the same bullshit when he was in school.

"Patti Carson t-boned him."

"Anybody hurt badly?"

"I think we got a broken arm. Some cuts and bruises. Patti bumped her head pretty good. She'll need stitches. But all in all, coulda been a helluva lot worse."

Pierce sighed. "Kid in the ambulance? He okay?"

"Well, Patrick Hoffman whacked his head on the driver's window. I think he'll need stitches. Kid with him in the passenger seat took the brunt of it."

Probably the broken arm, if there was one.

"Who is it?" he asked George. Not that it mattered, but it was a small area, and odds were, Pierce knew everybody on the road at the moment. He swung his gaze back over his shoulder to see Marlowe leaning on the side of his truck, watching and waiting.

"Don't know his name. New kid. Him and his mom been around the area for just a little bit."

George's answer piqued his curiosity. New kid. Marlowe had just told him about a new kid pounding Evan Church's nose in. Coincidence? They didn't get too many new kids in the area.

"Anything I can do?" he asked George.

"Covered. Thanks." George shook his head. "Talk some sense into the dumbass kids who think all this bullshit is fun."

"Yep." Pierce nodded. "I try."

He eyed the kid in the back of the ambulance as he headed back to his truck. Thin, a bit scrawny looking. His curly mop of dark hair was pushed back from a stark white face; his eyes looked hollow. Probably in shock. Definitely the new kid, because it wasn't Patrick Hoffman. Pierce wondered if this was the same kid who had fought with Evan Church earlier in the week. As if he could sense his stare, the kid jerked his gaze to lock eyes with Pierce.

"Everything okay?" Marlowe asked when he neared his truck.

"Yeah. Dumbass kids."

"Still up for pizza?"

"To hell with the pizza. I need a beer."

five

• • •

WY

Dec didn't look pathetic. He didn't look ashamed. Didn't appear to be lost in thought, wishing he would have made a different choice earlier tonight. In fact, even with his wrist and forearm in a cast, he didn't appear to be in that much pain. Her son simply wore that same sullen, impatient expression he had adopted back when he was still just a tween.

Wynona, on the other hand, was wrecked. From the moment she realized Declan had snuck out until getting the phone call from the sheriff's department telling her he had been involved in a car accident, she had dragged around her house—frantic and yet, weighted down with dread. Once she got the phone call, the dread burned into terror, worry, that Declan was injured far worse than what the deputy had said he was. The terror rode with her to Urgent Care, growing heavier with each mile.

She had walked into the clinic on weak knees, but the second she saw the familiar look on Dec's face, the terror had turned to fury. She had no idea what to do with her son, but she knew his bad behavior was escalating, and she had to take control now.

"Can we stop for pizza? On the way home?"

"Get in the car," she told him.

"I'm hungry."

Still shaking with rage, feeling chastised like a little girl herself—after the deputy lectured both her and Dec on the dangers of reckless driving—her stomach roiled and cramped as she marched around the SUV to get in the driver's side. Never mind that Declan wasn't driving; Wy had no doubt her son had either suggested to Patrick Hoffman that they play the ignorant game of driving with no headlights or stood one hundred percent behind the Hoffman kid's choice.

"The last thing I will do is get you pizza," she announced as she started the little SUV.

"Okay. Then what are you fixing for supper?"

Wy gripped the steering wheel in steady hands and took a deep breath. She wanted to smack him for the attitude. But she had never been one to do that to her son, not outside of a few mild spankings when he was a little boy. Exhausted, her head pounding now after the roller coaster of emotions that she had just ridden over the past couple of hours, she had no desire to go home and cook.

But damned if she would stop at the Black Olive and pick up pizza. It happened to be Dec's favorite place in Kissing Springs. The few times the two of them had gone there together, they'd enjoyed the pizza, and Wy had enjoyed time with her son. Not tonight, though.

"I'll go to the store and pick something up," she told him.

"You could get pizza with mushrooms and onions," he said quietly.

Still ready to blow up at her son for sneaking out, for the dangerous antics he and his friend had done in his car, Wy held her breath and peeked at her son. With his head turned just a bit to the passenger window, all she could see was his profile. The snotty-kid look was gone. Right now, he looked sad. Alone.

He hated mushrooms and onions.

Wy had to bite back a laugh, albeit a sad one.

"Dammit, Declan," she mumbled as she pried her fingers loose from the wheel and dropped a hand to the gearshift. "What am I gonna do with you?"

From the corner of her eye, she saw him lift and drop his shoulders in a dramatic shrug.

"Why did you sneak out?"

"Cuz you said I couldn't go anywhere. Living here is boring as fuck."

"Declan." She groaned and turned to look at him, exasperated with him all over again.

"Sorry." He ground the word out through gritted teeth. "I hate it here, Mom."

"You hated Sioux Falls, too," she reminded him.

"Least I had friends there."

"What about Mason?" She put the SUV in gear and pulled away from the curb in front of the clinic. "And why were you with Patrick Hoffman? Isn't he older than you?"

"He's a senior." His answer wasn't really an answer to her question, but Wy suspected he was avoiding her question on purpose.

"Earlier you said you were going to Mason's."

"I went to Mason's. Me 'n' another bunch of guys walked to Hoffman's house."

"Do you know how reckless, how stupid and irresponsible that was? Driving with no headlights on? Running a stop sign?"

"I wasn't driving," he reminded her.

"Declan." She leveled him with a look of frustration. "You were in the car. And you know driving a car is like handling a bullet. You could kill someone with a stunt like what you guys did earlier. You could kill yourself."

"Might not be so bad."

Wy tapped the brakes and mindful of possible traffic in the street behind her, she pulled the SUV over to the curb again.

"What did you say?"

Declan simply shook his head and refused to look at her.

"Declan, I love you. Dad loves you. We will get through this, okay?"

"Sure, Mom."

Now the roiling cocktail of emotion in her gut included guilt. She had wanted a child; when she and Zach found out they were expecting Declan, they had both been overjoyed. And she loved the kid to the moon and back. But maybe she didn't deserve to be a mother. She was doing a fine job of screwing up her kid's life. When Declan continued to stare out the passenger window, Wy took a deep breath and slumped forward to rest her forehead on the steering wheel.

"If he loves me, why did he let me come here with you?"

Zach Herzog did love Declan. Wynona knew that for certain. But she and Zach had burned the bridges between them all to hell, and even knowing her ex loved their son, she didn't want him raising him. It was bad enough in Declan's childhood years that he had witnessed the way she and Zach used to fight. The times Zach had gotten physical with her. She didn't want her very impressionable teenage son to stay in that environment and learn to deal with disappointment and anger with his fists.

Then again, maybe she was already too late.

She didn't have an answer for him. Instead, Wy sucked in another big breath and let it out slowly. She didn't count to three. Didn't envision a happy place; hell, she had no idea where that would be anyway. She had done therapy to death, more than she'd ever done Zach Herzog, that was certain. And still, she hadn't found the way to cope with all the ragged emotion she was carrying around.

Putting the car in gear again, she drove to the next stop sign and made a right. She was folding again, of course. She would get pizza, because now she felt guilty for the way her son was hurting. Zach had usually been the one to get violent, and yet, Wy had stayed far too long and let it go on too long. And then she had dragged her son away from the only home he had ever known.

To make herself feel better, she decided she would load the pizza down with every vegetable she could think of. She would make certain Dec knew she was getting the pizza to make things easier on herself, not for him.

six

. . .

PIERCE

In training, it was hammered into him and the other volunteer firefighters that no call was routine. Another key lesson—don't die for property. Pierce pulled his mask off now and stared at the burned-out hull of what used to be a garage on Main Street in Rodey. The automotive center—seemed kind of wishful thinking to Pierce, as Rodey probably didn't have fifty cars in town—had been closed for damned near as long as he could remember. After Wilbur Donnis closed up shop, nothing was done with the little shack. Cobwebs gathered. Rain washed them away. More cobwebs gathered. Mice made nests inside the place. Pierce didn't doubt other animals had taken up space in the run-down building. The wooden siding splintered and warped; windows were broken. And kids had decorated the building with so much graffiti, there might be a short story written on the exterior of the building.

Interesting that the little ramshackle building had stood for all those years with spray paint and animal excrement being the only thing done to or added to it. And now suddenly, someone decided to torch the place. Especially of interest to Pierce was how this incident had come on the heels of Patrick Hoffman's reckless driving accident two nights before—one in which a *new kid* was injured, and how the day before that, a *new kid* had broken Evan Church's nose.

Born and raised in Rodey, Pierce knew there weren't that many new kids in the entire damned *area* in a year's time. Which most likely meant that the new kid in those stories was one and the same. He sounded like a pain in the ass troublemaker, and Pierce suspected he was behind this fire.

Brian Rausch, the staging officer on scene, spoke into his radio, eyes still locked on the charred remains of the garage. Standing ten feet away, Pierce heard Bowman answer from the other side of the building. They'd had the fire under control relatively quickly; the flames were completely doused now. No injuries. This time.

Pierce heard the chatter of the small crowd that had gathered around the perimeter. He peeked over his shoulder, irritated by the audience. It was natural; he knew that. Even he did it; if he was in the grocery store and heard a siren, he would often wander outside to check things out. But he wasn't a looky-loo. He was a helper. Pierce had grown up with that need to lend a hand, to help anyone in need.

People that gathered at what could be tragedies irritated him. He rolled his eyes when he saw the Kissing Springs news van pull up. If anything topped his irritation with looky-loos, it was media. Determined to get away from the scene before a photographer snapped his picture or Amelia Reilly could catch him for an interview, Pierce headed back toward the first engine. He dragged his gaze over the small crowd again, this time noticing an unfamiliar face. Living in Rodey meant knowing just about every damned person not only in Rodey, but in all the surrounding small towns.

The woman's dark hair was pulled away from a pale, tight face. From the distance, he couldn't begin to guess her eyes color, but it would be hard to miss her sharp cheekbones and thin lips. The look of worry etched into her frown tugged at him. Forgetting the threat of media presence, Pierce turned and made his way back toward the crowd. The woman jerked her gaze from the garage to look at him as he neared her.

Now that he was closer, he noticed her eyes were the color of cognac. The thought, ridiculous as it was because brown was brown, stirred a thirst deep inside. A shot of Lockland bourbon would go down good right now. A little sip of the brunette would be appreciated too, but Pierce had a bad feeling about her.

Dressed in dark denim, knee-high chocolatey brown boots, and a camel-colored coat, she stuck out like a sore thumb. Most of the crowd around her was decked out in flannel and tennis shoes or hiking boots. Mrs. Franzen had her house slippers on. This woman looked like she had walked out of a catalog shoot to be here.

Her dark brow still furrowed, she tipped her head and parted her lips.

"Was anyone hurt?"

Her thick butterscotch voice brought to mind sweet honey and long, wet kisses in a shadowy room. Pierce gave himself a mental shake and reminded himself to focus.

"No." He shook his head. "Thankfully, no one was around."

Her nostrils flared as she drew in a deep breath and nodded, her attention going back to the burned building.

"You're new around here." His announcement seemed to startle her. She looked back at him again in askance. "What's your name?"

"Wynona Herzog." She spoke quietly, her voice fading considerably on her last name.

"Where's your son?" he pushed.

"I'm sorry?"

"Your son's the new kid causing trouble around town, isn't he?"

Wynona Herzog drew away from him like he had slapped her.

"Broke Evan Church's nose."

A tiny flinch told him he was right.

"And he was with Patrick Hoffman the other night when he wrecked his car."

"Declan wasn't driving."

"Declan," Pierce repeated. "You let *Declan* know I'm watching him."

"Excuse me?" Her tone was indignant, but anger fueled Pierce now. Her son had hurt his friend's kid, could have killed Patti Carson, and in all likelihood had just set a building on fire. Granted, the old building was empty and not much of a loss. But next time, it could be deadly.

And Pierce had no doubt there would be a next time.

"Where is he, Mrs. Herzog?" He narrowed his eyes at her. "Did Declan start this fire?"

"No." She answered without hesitation, without flinching. And yet, her eyes were haunted, and her lips were frozen in a tight line.

"You sure about that?"

"He's been at home with me all day," she answered in a clipped tone. "Working on a history paper."

Pierce nodded. "We'll see about that."

seven

. . .

WY

"Hey."

The female bartender called out to her with a smile when Wynona stepped inside the Skeleton Bar. She had been working all morning, but she was so desperate for a break, for human contact, she finally gave up and climbed into her SUV. Remembering then that she was in the middle of nowhere, Kentucky, she had googled a place to grab some lunch. Sure, she and Dec had been here for a little while, but Wy hadn't ventured out much on her own yet.

Today, she needed it. Her brain was still reeling from all the craziness of the weekend. The incident with Dec and the kid fighting in school. The kid's mom calling with a threat about pressing charges. The car accident and Dec's broken arm.

The way that damned burly-looking jerk firefighter had approached her last night out of the fucking blue and pointed his finger at Declan for starting that fire.

The hell of it was, if Dec hadn't been sitting in their tiny, postage-stamped size kitchen all damned day, she wouldn't put it past him to go looking for trouble like that. And that pissed her off. Working from home had been a godsend in the beginning, but after trying to shove all this stress aside and stewing over it anyway all morning, Wy left the house, ready to make friends with squirrels or skunks.

She would get a damned dog to cuddle up to, but she didn't need another mouth to feed, another soul to take care of.

Nope. Just once, Wy wished someone would take care of her.

"Hi." She smiled at the bartender as she crossed the trendy room to the bar. "Okay to sit here?"

"Of course," the woman answered with a quick nod. "I'm Bristol."

"Wynona." She cleared her throat as she climbed up to sit on a barstool.

"What sounds good?" Bristol asked her. Dressed in jeans and a green sweatshirt that said *Lockland Distilling* on the front chest, the woman appeared to be right at home here. Wy swallowed the taste of envy. She couldn't remember the last time she had felt at home anywhere.

"A bottle of Lockland Five Year," she mumbled, "but I'll settle for a glass of iced tea."

"Sweet tea?" Bristol's toned-down question, the enthusiasm gone and replaced by understanding—not pity, Wynona hoped—drew her attention from her bag as she set it on the bar in front of her. Thankfully, Bristol was still smiling; if anything, her face seemed to say *I get it,* rather than a look of *you're having a shit day, what can I do for you?* Similar, yes, and yet these days, there was a huge difference to Wy, and the pity thing made her prickly as a fucking pear.

"No," she shook her head and pressed the tips of her fingers to her closed eyes. "Unsweetened, please."

"You got it." Bristol nodded and laid something down on the bar in front of Wy. When she was sure she was alone, Wynona dropped her hands and opened her eyes to find a green leather menu. She flipped it open, even though she wasn't hungry. She had to eat something. She'd lost fifteen pounds the last few months, and she wasn't trying. Just too damned hard to shove food down to her belly when it was so full of emotion.

Still, she needed to eat. She had work to do when she got home, and she couldn't keep dropping pounds and inches. One day Dec would get home from school and not be able to find her.

Intrigued by the idea for a moment, by the thought of disappearing, Wy zoned out. She had loved Zach Herzog once upon a time. Looking back now, she couldn't remember why. What she had loved about him. The only good thing he had ever given her was their son. And fifteen years later, they were well on their way to fucking up his life, too.

"Want to order some lunch?" Bristol reappeared with a glass of iced tea.

"No." Wy laughed softly. "But I need to."

"Can I make a suggestion?"

"Please do."

"Cup of beer cheese soup and half a turkey sandwich."

The words made her mouth water.

"Okay." She nodded.

"Holler if you need anything." Bristol told her as she headed behind the back bar, most likely to put in Wy's order.

Alone again for a moment, Wy pulled her phone from her purse, almost afraid to look at it. What if she had a missed phone call from school? What if Dec was already in trouble again this week? It was only Monday. Only October. He was only a sophomore. She had so much mothering left to do, and she was at her wits' end.

And yet, the idea of Declan growing up, graduating, moving away—all of that terrified her, too. Not even because she worried he wasn't clear on right and wrong, but because she knew somehow that if he moved away from her, she would most likely never see him again. It wasn't that she thought he would go back to South Dakota, to his father. Rather, Wy suspected once Dec turned eighteen, he would hotfoot it the hell away from her and Zach and go it alone.

And yes, from there, likely end up in trouble.

She would miss him.

Didn't matter what kind of future she envisioned for her son; it broke her heart to think about it.

"You okay?"

Clearing her throat, she blinked back tears before looking at Bristol again.

"Yeah." She shrugged and licked her lips. "Just having a Monday."

"Familiar with Mondays myself," Bristol answered. "Passing through?"

"No. My son and I moved here a few months ago."

"Oh."

Wy flinched at Bristol's a-ha tone, but the woman was still smiling.

"Okay. I knew someone new had settled in the area," Bristol continued. "Welcome to Rodey."

"Thank you."

"I moved here a few years ago. From Indiana."

Wynona noticed the diamond solitaire on her finger, but she didn't ask. Instead, she simply rubbed her thumb over the bottom of her naked ring finger. She'd shoved her wedding ring at Zach once, in one of their last fights. True to his hateful self, he had laughed in her face and told her to keep it. He didn't want it, and it wasn't worth a hundred bucks. The taunt had landed hard, taking her breath away. Zach had given her the ring when she was nineteen. She had known he hadn't gone to a jeweler and dropped thousands in cash, but the ring was pretty. The diamond a decent size. Not to mention the sweet, romantic way he had proposed to her.

She had put the ring away, locked it in a jewelry box when she and Dec left Sioux Falls. Assuming Zach bought it at a discount store, or that it wasn't even a diamond, she never considered pawning it. But she had no desire to ever look at it again.

Bristol was still standing there, apparently interested in conversation. Exactly what Wy had needed when she stormed out of her little rental house earlier. And yet, now that she was here, she couldn't force herself to talk. It wasn't that she thought Zach would get in his ridiculous souped-up truck and come after and beat her senseless. Their violence had been more controlled than that. And the divorce had put an end to all that nonsense.

She thought.

Still. There was a tiny part of her that worried he might come after her one day. She hadn't bothered to hide her tracks. She didn't know where to obtain fake IDs for her and Declan. And honestly, she didn't think she wanted to keep Dec from Zach. But she wasn't sure.

About any damned thing. How the hell had she been more sure of herself as a teenager than she was now?

"Sioux Falls," she said quietly.

"South Dakota."

"Mmm." Wy nodded. "Have you been there?"

"No." Bristol shook her head. "Maybe someday."

"What brought you here? When you left Indiana?"

Wy held her breath, waiting for Bristol to tell her to mind her own business. But Bristol only shifted on her feet and leaned to rest on the bar.

"Well." She frowned. "I found the job here. And I left on a whim."

"You left a guy?"

"I did." She nodded. "The thing was it took him a while to realize I was really gone."

"Did he come looking for you?"

At this, Bristol laughed softly. "Oh, he did. Things got complicated."

Wy picked her tea up for a sip. "You're with him now?" She couldn't help but look at the ring on Bristol's hand.

"No." Bristol shook her head. "He, um…well, he followed me here. I was already wrapped up in someone else. So, my ex… ended up with someone else here."

"Oh." Wy frowned. That would be hell. She couldn't imagine Zach moving here, even if she had nothing to do with him. Even if she was safe from his anger and his fists. "I don't think I could do that."

"Married?" Bristol asked her.

"Divorced."

Wy felt her shoulders tense as she waited for Bristol to fire another question at her. Eventually, she would ask about Declan. Had she heard about the trouble Declan had been in? Would she make the connection? The way that firefighter had last night?

"Well." She smiled as she straightened. "You need to meet my friends."

"I'm not interested in dating anyone—"

"Not talking about dating." Bristol shook her head. "Girlfriends. Reading club. Wine drinking. Softball league."

All of the above sounded appealing to Wy. Except maybe softball. She was athletic as a rock.

"Let me check on your order," Bristol told her. Wy's phone buzzed on the bar as Bristol slipped away again. Holding her breath, Wy picked the phone up and peeked at the screen. She nearly collapsed with relief when she saw that it was a work email and not a phone call.

She did need friends. Never mind that she hardly remembered how to talk to friends, how to go out and have a glass of wine or read a book for fun. Never mind that her life now was aches and pains, some arthritis from old broken bones, work, and raising a rebellious teenager, praying she made it through one day at a time with her kid staying out of trouble.

eight

. . .

PIERCE

Branch Lockland nodded at him as he rolled a dolly stacked high with boxes into the back of the bar.

"You seen Summer?" Branch hollered across the parking lot.

"Nope."

"Tell her I need to talk to her if you do."

Pierce waved in agreement and let the door close behind him. Branch's sister Summer was supposed to be taking it easy, working from home, cutting back her hours. However it was phrased, Summer wasn't doing it. Pierce was surprised she had stayed home for the full ten weeks of her maternity leave last spring, but she had. He had still seen a lot of her. For one thing, he and Summer's husband Taj were friends. But also, Summer's family owned Lockland Distilling and the Skeleton Bar, where Pierce worked his day job.

Bristol had country music playing in the bar right now. Pierce nodded his head in time to the beat of the "Last Night" though he refused to sing along. No one within hearing distance deserved to hear him butcher Morgan Wallen's song. Ballcap backwards on his head and his t-shirt wet with sweat, he wheeled the dolly into the little storeroom.

"Got some Lockland Single Barrell for you, Bristol!" he hollered. Odds were, she wouldn't hear him. It was early afternoon, and they weren't often busy at this hour. Definitely not on Mondays. But Bristol always found something to do, so she might be up on a ladder right at this moment cleaning ceiling tiles with a toothbrush for all he knew. Not surprised when she didn't answer him, he unloaded the boxes to the floor and then pulled a box knife from the pocket of his cargo pants.

He heard her voice out front as he sliced through the packing tape on the top box. Normally, he wouldn't worry about opening the boxes immediately, but because he had tended bar Saturday evening, he knew they needed the single barrel bottles up front.

"Here ya go…" he called, a bottle in both hands, as he made his way out of the storeroom and behind the bar. His voice trailed off when he realized Bristol was talking to someone. A customer, not a fellow employee. "Bristol."

"Nice!" She turned and flashed him a small smile. "Just chattin' up a new friend. C'mere."

Pierce set the bottles down and meandered down the polished wooden bar to stand beside Bristol. Turning his attention to the woman on the opposite side of the bar, Pierce felt his shoulders lock with tension. It was the woman from last night. At the scene of the garage fire.

"Wynona Herzog." He tipped his head and arched his eyebrows. Though he was surprised to see her, Pierce wasn't surprised that Bristol was chatting her up. Just one of the reasons Bristol made a damned good bar manager. Never mind that she had a good mind for business. She was good with people.

"You two know each other?" she asked with a grin, and then she immediately shook her head. "Why am I surprised? This is Rodey, Kentucky."

"We've met," Pierce answered and nodded. He took his time looking at Wynona Herzog. She wore her dark hair in loose, long waves today. A wine-colored turtleneck sweater with weird but cool looking drapey sleeves. Pierce figured there was a name for the style, but he couldn't be bothered to care. The bag on the counter was designer but looking closely he could see a bit of wear in the black leather.

"Is that what you call it?" Wynona quirked an eyebrow at him, apparently amused. "When you approach me at the scene of a fire and accuse my son of starting said fire?"

Pierce flinched. He wasn't exactly sorry, but *he was wrong*. As far as he was concerned, he and everyone else in Rodey had every right to be suspicious of Declan Herzog. But one of the deputies had taken a statement from a guy who had seen another guy light the garage on fire. Pierce didn't have all the details, but he did know the guys who had been arrested were drifters, supposedly on their way through town from the Virginia side of the state to some unnamed city in Missouri.

Could be bullshit.

Declan Herzog could have started that fire.

But he wouldn't press the issue. Not now.

"Pierce Rooney." Bristol turned fierce eyes on him. Okay, so maybe everyone else but Bristol would be suspicious of Wynona's son. And Summer. Summer wouldn't be suspicious.

Or Sheridan, Summer's sister-in-law.

Hell, the women in Rodey were tight. If they adopted Wynona Herzog into their circle, there'd be hell to pay if he looked at her or her son wrong.

"Did she tell you what her son did at school last week?" He glanced at Bristol, but from the corner of his eye, he saw Wynona wince. He almost felt bad, but then he remembered Evan Church's splinted and packed nose.

"Remember what you did to Rye Gallaher when y'all were in high school?"

Pierce's mouth dropped open in shock. Bristol had only moved to Rodey a few years ago; she hadn't been around when he was in high school.

"Who the hell told you about that?"

"Small town, Pierce," she reminded him.

"You didn't grow up here!" he argued.

He glanced at Wynona when he saw movement in his peripheral vision. She had picked up her glass to take a drink of what looked like tea.

"No, but I see Chantele every week."

Well, of course, Rye's live-in girlfriend would know the story about Pierce and Rye fighting in gym class. Over a girl. About Pierce giving Rye a black eye and a split lip. Never mind that Rye had landed a solid punch to Pierce's ribs.

Bristol turned back to Wynona.

"Did he seriously accuse your son of starting the fire at Wilbur's garage?"

To her credit, Wynona didn't give Bristol a real answer. She simply glanced at him and stared at him with a look that said drop dead.

"Declan and I spent the day jammed together in a kitchen about the size of your bathroom here," Wynona announced. "He was working on a history paper about the Vietnam War. I was working right beside him all day."

"Don't be a dick," Bristol muttered as she gave Pierce the side eye.

Even though he would still be suspicious of the kid, Pierce felt like he owed Wynona an apology.

"I apologize for what I said. Someone's been arrested for starting that fire."

Beside him, Bristol rolled her eyes.

"Pierce is a volunteer firefighter. This is his day job."

"I'll remember that," Wynona announced as she reached for her purse.

"Great." Bristol turned his way and lobbed a soft, fake punch at him. "Go away. You don't need to be running my friends off."

Pierce sighed. "You seen Summer? Branch is looking for her."

"She was out back at the amphitheater with Knox last time I saw her."

nine

. . .

PIERCE

"Has Mom heard from Lyndi at all?"

Pierce peeked at his dad over the counter, not wanting to catch his eyes, but curious about his reaction.

"She called a few nights ago."

The vague answer told him nothing. Had Mom called Lyndi? Or had Lyndi called?

"She doing okay?"

"Ready to quit her job," his dad answered as he stacked several pickles on a sandwich. "Sure you don't want one?"

"Already ate," Pierce answered. He looked around the kitchen where he had grown up. His parents had remodeled when he was fourteen; sometimes, he still missed the old room. The small area, almost too tight for their kitchen table. The floral wallpaper. The old harvest gold gas range. Now the room was at least three times the size, as his parents had opted to take out a wall and open the area to the dining room.

Pierce understood. It was their house; they had sacrificed on things for years to give him and his sister everything, and now they had the right to do what they wanted, make changes, spruce things up. Hell, they had the right to sell the place and move to Florida if they wanted to.

They had talked about it.

"Mom's ready to quit her job?" he asked now, a bit surprised. What if they had talked about it enough that they'd decided to do it? His dad was retired; he had spent years in the agriculture business. He could move anywhere he wanted to now and do any kind of odds and ends job he chose. Or he could play golf and lounge on a beach all day.

"Lyndi is." His dad huffed as he shot Pierce a look as if to say keep up or get real. Pierce watched him screw the lid back on the pickle jar and put his sandwich fixings in the refrigerator. "I think she's homesick."

"What makes you say that?"

"She mentioned wanting to come home."

"Lyndi in Rodey, Kentucky is a little bit like Old Man Turner in Buckingham Palace, Dad." Pierce rolled his eyes.

"Not necessarily."

"Lyndi is too big for Rodey," he continued. His dad hesitated at the refrigerator and finally tugged the door open again. He grabbed a longneck bottle and offered it to Pierce. "She hated it here. She didn't mix."

"Maybe so." His dad selected another longneck bottle, bumped the fridge closed, and picked up his plate. Pierce followed him into his man cave—another new feature in his parents' house. It used to be Pierce's bedroom. "Or maybe she just thought that. And she left to try something, somewhere, new, and it wasn't for her."

"She called me last week."

"Lyndi did?" His dad put his dinner on an end table and rooted in the drawer of said table for the remote control. He aimed it at the big screen TV on the wall. Pierce expected ESPN, but his dad selected Netflix and chose some kind of spy TV series. Season four of eight. He had no idea his dad was into binge-watching TV.

"Where's Mom again?"

"Book club," his dad answered.

"Since when?"

"For the past year." His dad gave him a look. "She and some other ladies meet and discuss books and drink wine."

"Mm-hmm." Pierce rolled his eyes.

"Oh, they do." His dad laughed. "They rotate houses. Sure, they get into the bottles, but those women like to tear into a book, too."

Pierce, assuming they read things like *Fifty Shades of Gray*, scrambled to change the subject.

"Lyndi was upset when she called me."

"About what?" His dad picked up the remote again and muted the volume on the recap of the previous episode.

"I think she was at the library. A group of women or girls was bothering her. She was afraid to walk out alone."

"That right there might be why she wants to come home."

"Dad." Pierce sighed. "Why would a group of women go after Lyndi?"

"Who the hell knows why anyone would do anything, Pierce? Maybe she dated one of them, and things ended badly. Maybe it was a revenge thing."

"Lyndi is dating women now?"

"I have no idea!" his dad bellowed. "I'm sure she's fine. She's young. Let her live."

Pierce didn't give a rat's ass about who his sister dated, as long as she wasn't in danger.

"You and Mom still talking about moving to Florida?"

Rather than look at his dad, he picked at a hangnail.

"Dunno."

Did his dad know anything? Probably best not to ask that. Pierce twisted the top off his bottle and took a long swig.

"We might go visit for a while. After the holidays."

"Visit?" Pierce shook his head when his dad looked at him.

"Florida."

"What holidays?"

"Maybe between Thanksgiving and Christmas. Maybe after Christmas."

"Son-of-bitch." Pierce laughed. "You're doin' it, aren't ya? Moving?"

"I don't know. Your mother really thinks she wants a condo on the beach."

"What about hurricanes?"

His dad shrugged. "She counters with tornadoes."

"What do you want, Dad?"

"I want whatever will make your mom happy, Pierce." His dad took a big bite of his sandwich and chewed thoughtfully. "The thing is, if your mom and I move, it leaves a place here for Lyndi."

Pierce nodded. "So you wouldn't sell the house?"

Somehow that made him feel a bit better about the idea of them moving. At least there would still be a homebase here in Rodey.

"Nothing's been decided for sure."

"Is Lyndi planning to be home for Thanksgiving?"

"Far as I know."

Pierce swallowed another drink as his dad unmuted the TV. They watched in silence for a few minutes. Didn't seem like a bad show, but Pierce was already involved in his own series. He would have to remember this one when he finished the last season of his cop show.

"What book is Mom's group talking about this month?"

He braced himself, ready to hear some sexy, schmexy title.

"*The Southern Book Club's Guide to Vampire Slaying*. I think."

Pierce blinked at his dad and finally nodded.

"She says it's some kind of commentary on feminism."

"Okay, then."

ten

• • •

WY

She hadn't braved it and gone back to the Skeleton Bar. As much as she had enjoyed talking to Bristol, Wynona had no desire to run into that Pierce guy again. Even if he had admitted someone had been arrested for staring that garage fire. Even if he had apologized to her for targeting Declan the night of the fire. He might have sounded somewhat sincere, but he had looked at her as if he needed her to know he still didn't trust her.

Or more to the point, her son.

Wynona knew it wouldn't matter what happened; if there was any trouble in the area in the days to come, Pierce Rooney would come after Dec. Bristol had reassured her once he walked away that day in the bar that he was a good guy. Maybe he was. And maybe he was right to look at her son with suspicion. But Wy had no desire to spend any amount of time with the guy, not with any guy, actually. Not after finally getting away from Zach.

But after another week of solitude broken only by an occasional semi-fun conversation with Dec and a hundred little digs and arguments with the kid, Wy was desperate for company. Sadly, she didn't trust Declan to behave himself, so she would never have a night life—even if that night life only consisted of book club meetings or hanging with the girls. Any time she took for herself, Wy would have to do through the day, once she had her work caught up and Declan was at school.

Even with the possibility of running into Pierce, with the long week behind her and nothing but more long days and nights ahead, Wy decided to take a chance and go to lunch at the Skeleton Bar again. She could drive in to Kissing Springs; there were some cute places there. French Kiss Coffee was one of her favorite places, and if she wanted a grilled ham and cheese with fries, Hope's Diner was a sure bet. But Wy wasn't looking for food—she could whip up her own ham and cheese sandwich if that were the case.

Nope. Wy wanted to talk to Bristol. She would be happy to sit in the bar and watch Bristol clean the bar and mix drinks. They could share meaningless conversation about the best all-purpose cleaner or how to make pecan pie. Wy just wanted some inane chatter to break up the monotony of her days.

As was the case last Monday, the parking lot at the Skeleton Bar wasn't packed. Wynona figured the busy days for a distillery and bourbon bar were more midweek to the weekend. Served her just fine. While she was desperate for conversation, she didn't love the idea of being swallowed up by a crowd.

Unfortunately, Bristol was nowhere in sight when she stepped inside the bar today. Pierce Rooney stood with his back to the door, studying something on the back bar. Soft, country music played from hidden speakers. Two older men sat at the far end of the bar, deep in conversation. And three tables were occupied.

Pierce turned as she stood there, undecided about staying or leaving. Too late to slip out unnoticed, Wy trudged across the floor to the same stool she had claimed last Monday. To his credit, Pierce greeted her with what appeared to be a warm, sincere smile.

"Hey." He rested his hands on the bar and tipped his head at her as she climbed up to sit. "Wynona."

"Pierce." She nodded. Frustrated that she hadn't considered this might happen, Wy sighed and arched her eyebrows. She wouldn't ask for Bristol. Nope, she was a big girl. She could order lunch and read something on her phone while she ate. Maybe she wouldn't get the conversation she was looking for, but at least the Skeleton Bar was different scenery for a while.

"Lunch menu?" he asked. His voice was friendly, but Wy was still wary about talking to him.

"Please."

He nodded and moved to grab the green leather menu from a small pile a few feet away on the bar. His movements were fluid and easy, as if he worked the bar often. Silly Wynona had just assumed when Bristol said he worked at the bar that he was a behind-the-scenes kind of guy. She should have known better. Her luck dictated that she would run into this guy on a regular basis now.

"Iced tea?"

Eyes on the menu as he handed it to her, Wy froze, surprised by his question. Chin still tipped to her chest, she raised her gaze to look at him.

"Sweet or unsweet?" he asked when she nodded.

"Unsweet." Her voice was no more than a whisper when she answered him.

"I'll grab that and give you a minute to look at the menu," he told her.

She nodded again, but rather than look at the menu, she watched him as he turned away from her and grabbed a glass. His dark green button-up shirt accentuated his broad shoulders. Wy watched his back as he filled the glass with ice and poured her tea. His short dirty blond hair was neatly trimmed; his sideburns a throwback look that Wynona had never been attracted to.

Before now.

He wore dark jeans with the green Lockland shirt, the tail untucked but still somehow neat. She couldn't see his shoes, but she knew they would be something fashionable. Definitely not the boots he had been wearing the night of the fire. The night he had come at her accusing her son of arson.

She sucked in a quick breath when he turned to catch her staring.

Doesn't matter how good-looking he is. He was in your face less than ten days ago, slinging bold accusations at your son.

"Let me guess," he said with a wicked grin. Wy held her breath, assuming he was about to make a comment about how she couldn't keep her eyes off him. About the fit of his jeans or something ridiculous about his firefighter body. "You're watching me instead of reading the menu in case I decided to be an ass and give you sweet tea."

Genuinely surprised by his comment, she couldn't help a small laugh.

"No." She shook her head. "No."

"I'm not," he told her as he set the glass down in front of her.

"Not what?"

"An ass," he said with a self-deprecating smile and shrug. "I know we got off on the wrong foot—"

"You accused my son of starting a building on fire," she reminded him. "I'd hardly call that starting off on the wrong foot."

Pierce winced and nodded. "I did. And I apologized, if you remember."

Throat dry under his intense stare, Wy reached for her tea and took a sip.

"Didn't feel all that sincere," she mumbled.

"Fire's a dangerous mistress," he said quietly. "Intoxicating as hell. But it can be deadly."

Eyes locked, Wy's heartbeat quickened.

"My son's not dangerous," she answered, mostly to remind herself that she didn't like this guy. Because he had verbally and unjustly attacked her child.

"Maybe not." He tipped his head again. "Maybe not on purpose. But he is a kid. And sometimes kids make bad decisions."

He said it like he was experienced in bad decisions. Or maybe in kids making bad decisions. Was he referring to whatever it was Bristol had brought up last Monday when she was here? Or maybe he had kids and understood how challenging parenting could be.

Wy jerked her gaze from his, and even though she told herself not to, she swept her gaze over his arms and hands to see he wasn't wearing a wedding ring.

Which didn't mean a damned thing.

Then again, maybe he was simply speaking from experience as a firefighter. Maybe there were often stupid, dangerous escapades out here in the middle of nowhere. Kids were kids across the country, and kids did make bad choices. It was part of growing up.

"What sounds good for lunch?" he asked her after a moment of silence between them. Wy heard a Reba McEntire song start, her damned brain got caught up in the lyrics, and finally she had to give herself a mental shake. If she didn't order, he would be standing here looking at her all-damned day.

"Chicken club sandwich."

"Good choice," he agreed. But then, why wouldn't he agree? He worked here. "Fries?"

"Sweet potato fries."

"Perfect. I'll get your order in."

Because she had been raised to be polite, she mumbled a thank you as he walked toward the back of the bar toward what she assumed was the kitchen.

eleven

. . .

PIERCE

He hadn't missed the look of disappointment on Wynona Herzog's face when he turned and saw her standing just inside the Skeleton Bar. Obviously, she hadn't come here looking for him. Most likely, she had hoped to find Bristol behind the bar. Pierce couldn't blame her for that. Everyone loved Bristol; she radiated positive energy.

Even though Pierce still wouldn't trust Wynona Herzog's son, he did feel bad for jumping the gun and flinging that baseless accusation at her the night of the garage fire. Obviously, the kid was trouble; how could anyone deny it after the fist fight with Evan Church? Same with the accident last weekend. However, Pierce wasn't dumb enough to believe that Evan Church was an angel just because he was friends with the kid's mom.

Patrick Hoffman could be trouble sometimes, too. That kid was hell bent on prison time. Wynona Herzog would do well to keep her kid away from the Hoffman kid.

She was looking at her phone when he brought her lunch plate out to her. Her brows were drawn in a deep frown. Pierce wondered if she was angry or worried, but he didn't have time to muse over it as she looked up when she sensed him coming.

"Thank you." She nodded and put her phone down when he put the plate on the bar.

"Everything okay?" he asked quietly.

"Yes. Thanks." She picked up her silverware and unwrapped the napkin. Pierce figured she thought he was asking about her order. After all, why would a jackass firefighter who accused her son of starting fires care about her well-being?

"Bristol's here today."

His words obviously caught her off-guard. She jerked her gaze up, frown firmly in place, and tipped her head.

"She's in a meeting with Summer," he explained. "But she should be back pretty quick."

"Okay." Wynona shrugged.

"I know you didn't walk in here today looking for me."

To his surprise, she barked a loud, harsh laugh.

"No, I didn't."

"How old is he?"

"Declan?"

"Your son." He nodded.

"Fifteen."

Pierce flinched. "Boys are hard."

"Don't patronize me, Pierce Rooney."

"Not my intention," he promised her. "I was a fifteen-year-old boy once."

Wynona picked up a fry without looking away from him.

"Yeah? You ever get accused of arson?"

Pierce clenched his teeth and shook his head. "No, ma'am. And I am sorry for that."

"Don't call me ma'am."

Prickly. He liked it.

And damned if he didn't admire her for defending her son. Especially in the wake of the kid's bad behavior just before the fire.

"What should I call you?"

"My friends call me Wy."

Pierce chuckled. "Maybe I look dumb, but I'm not gonna fall for that."

"Wynona." She shrugged.

"Wynona, enjoy your lunch. Please holler if there's anything else I can get you."

She stared at him a moment longer and finally dropped her gaze to her food.

"Ketchup?"

"Can do." He slipped halfway down the bar and snagged a ketchup bottle. Wynona thanked him when he handed it to her.

"Why do you do it?" she asked as he started to walk away again.

"Do what?"

"Firefighting. If this is your job, why do you do that?"

"Well, someone's got to," he said easily. "All these little towns out here far away from the big city fire stations."

"But you like it."

"I do." He nodded. "In fact, I had plans to move to Lexington. I wanted to be a firefighter in a bigger city."

"Why didn't you?"

Pierce watched her cut her sandwich into fourths.

"Careful," he warned. "You start asking me those kinds of questions, that's a greenlight for me to ask 'em back."

"Is that a threat?"

"That's polite conversation here in Rodey, Kentucky."

Pierce caught himself before he leaned on the bar. It would put him in her space, and Wynona Herzog didn't seem like the kind of woman who would want him in her space.

"I didn't leave Rodey," he told her, "because I got on here. The Locklands are good people. Good to work for. The benefits are good. And because I wanted to be around for my parents."

Pierce had spent six months in Lexington when he was fresh out of college. While he liked it there, met new people and remained in touch with most of them to this day, Lyndi had been a handful for his parents. She had been every bit the wild child he was when he was in school, only maybe worse. When his mom started having anxiety attacks, when his dad mistook the first severe anxiety attack for a heart attack, Pierce had gone back home. Maybe some would call him a coward, say that he used his family as an excuse to go home because he was homesick. Lexington wasn't far enough away for him to feel homesick, but Pierce had never been one to care what anyone thought of him.

Others, he knew, would roll their eyes at him for coming back home, as if just his presence in Rodey would make Lyndi behave or keep his mom calm. Neither had happened right off the bat, and maybe, neither had ever really happened. Because his sister had ended up leaving Rodey so she could be herself somewhere else, and his mom was still prone to anxiety attacks.

But he liked being close to his family.

"Are they well?"

"They are." He nodded. "Thank you for asking."

"Were you ever diagnosed with ODD?"

Pierce blinked at her, shocked by the question. "Have I ever been diagnosed with Oppositional Defiant Disorder? No."

Rather than explain the bizarre question, Wynona finally took a bite of her sandwich.

"Are you telling me your son has ODD?"

"No." She covered her mouth with her fingertips and shook her head. "No. I've just done some reading on it."

Pierce clenched his teeth together again to make sure he didn't say anything stupid. And in his mind, responding in any way to her comment would be stupid.

"How long have you lived here?" he asked instead.

"We moved this summer."

"Have you met many people?"

She laughed again as she chewed another bite. "Bristol. And if phone calls count, I met Amy Church recently."

Pierce cleared his throat. If he knew Amy, she had called to issue a warning. Most likely, another incident would mean she and her husband would press charges against Declan Herzog. Then again, another incident might do more damage to Declan than Evan, and Wynona could make the same threat.

"You need to meet Summer Lock—Bailey. Summer Bailey. Sheridan Kennedy. Marlowe—"

"Are they friends of Bristol's?"

"They are."

"And friends of yours?"

He grinned apologetically. "Small town life."

"Great." She patted her mouth with her napkin and took a sip of her tea.

"Are you married?"

"Why do you ask?"

Pierce held his hands up, palms out, in surrender. "Just curious. I'm not hitting on you."

He wasn't. But if they had gotten off to a different kind of start, he might ask her out. If she was single.

"No, you're curious because of Declan."

"Come again?"

"You're wondering if both of his parents are in the picture. Maybe thinking if I'm such a bad mother, he should live with his dad."

"Whoa. Whoa. Whoa." Pierce took a step back and shook his head. "No, ma'am. That's not at all why I asked. I'm just curious. You just asked me why I like to fight fires."

"And you never answered me."

"I think fire is mesmerizing," he answered simply. "I love the flames and the heat. As long as we get it all under control. She's a mean bitch when she gets out of hand."

Wynona quirked her eyebrows at him, but she didn't respond.

"Better to fight the fires than start them, right?" He shrugged.

She cleared her throat and looked away. The buzz of attraction hummed through Pierce's body as he watched her struggle to avoid eye contact with him. He rarely answered that particular question so honestly. In fact, Pierce wasn't sure he had ever said those words out loud. Usually, when someone asked why he was willing to charge into a burning building when everyone else was running from said building, his answer was a simple *to give back to my community*.

True.

And yet, what he had just confessed to Wynona Herzog was *his* truth—that deep-seated, hard kernel of truth that might horrify most people he knew. Hence his keeping it to himself.

"I'm divorced," she mumbled.

twelve

• • •

WY

Her shoulders slumped in relief when Pierce left her alone. He told her again to let him know if she needed anything else, but Wynona wouldn't ask him for a thing. Her belly still fluttered with nerves or fear as she munched on her lunch.

No. Not fear.

Nerves, maybe.

She wasn't sure she liked the guy, but damn did she like looking at him. His intense blue eyes tracking her every move made her heart race. They were mesmerizing. The same as he had said about fires. That conversation had been a bit terrifying, for more reason than one. Not the least of which being she knew somehow without him saying so that he didn't share his *attraction* to flames, to fire, with many people.

That knife of honesty that he had drawn over her heart left her breathless. And afraid. Not that Pierce would turn to arson for kicks and giggles. But because he had bared a tiny piece of his soul to her, and she had no doubt he would expect the same from her.

Sure, she had told him she was divorced, but that was common knowledge. He would have found that out eventually. Wy worried that one day, the big, sexy man with the pretty blue eyes would come back around and demand a secret in exchange for the one he had given her.

"Hey!" Bristol's happy greeting drew her from her thoughts. Wynona looked over her shoulder as the woman approached the bar. She tossed a casual arm around Wy's shoulders and gave her a gentle squeeze. "How're you today?"

"Good."

And she was. Declan had been moody this past week, but as far as she knew, he hadn't made any dangerous or stupid decisions since the night he broke his arm. Zach had texted her just a few moments ago, when Pierce had walked away. No ranting and raving, just asking how Dec was doing. She would have to call him later, so most likely her day would go south. But at least the text exchanges the past several days had been okay. She had called him the night she and Dec got home with their pizza—loaded with so many vegetables, there was no way Declan had managed to pick them all off. Zach hadn't answered, so she had left him a message about the accident, promising that the broken arm was the worst of it.

And just now, she had survived a short conversation with Pierce Rooney. True, they hadn't talked often, but after he accused Declan of starting that fire, she had come to think of him as her one enemy here in Rodey.

"You?" she asked when Bristol had come around to the service side of the bar.

"Good." The woman's smile was that same warm, friendly one Wy remembered. "Just had a meeting with Summer. She'll be over in a few for lunch. I'll introduce you."

Wy finished half of her sandwich, decided to save the other half for tomorrow's lunch, and continued to pick at her fries.

"I hope Mr. Rooney was polite today."

Wynona looked up with a snort. "He was fine."

"He really is a nice guy," Bristol promised her. "In fact, the only guy I'd advise you to stay away from around here is Mav Pressey. And he's not a bad guy. He just goes through women like most people drink water."

"Noted." Wy nodded.

"Bristol, are you sure you don't want me around tomorrow?"

Bristol arched her brow at Wynona as she looked toward the door. Her face lit up at the sight of whomever had just hollered at her.

"No." She rolled her eyes. "Stay home and take your baby trick-or-treating!"

"Beckett has two teeth. I think he'll be okay if we don't trick—"

"Summer." Bristol shook her head as a blonde walked around to join her on the service side of the bar. "Put Beckett in that adorable Dalmatian puppy costume and go visit all your people. You're gonna have a blast with Ellery and Stella, too. I can handle a Halloween party here."

The blonde grinned at Wynona and arched her eyebrows.

"He will be a pretty adorable puppy."

"See?" Bristol rolled her eyes again. "Take lots of pictures. That is your only job. Be with your son, the girls, and your husband."

"Okay." Summer tossed her hands up in surrender.

"Wynona, this is Summer Bailey."

"Oh, man, I love that." Summer flashed a grin at Wynona.

"Still in the newlywed phase," Bristol explained. "Summer, Wynona Herzog. She and her son moved to Rodey recently."

"Hi." Summer reached over the bar to shake Wy's hand. "Do you play softball?"

"No." Wynona snorted. "The best thing I can do for your team would be stay far away from the field."

"I'll show you how to keep score," Summer said with a smile.

"So, we're having a Halloween party here tomorrow night. Costumes are optional."

"Sounds fun." Wy shrugged. "But I can't."

"Your son?" Bristol asked.

"How old is he?" Summer turned away to fill a glass with ice.

"Fifteen."

"Mmm." She nodded. "I have three older brothers. I think they were always in trouble of some kind."

"I think we're nearing boys-will-be-boys territory here."

Summer nodded at Bristol. "Maybe. But girls will be girls. I had some fun when I was younger."

"You're having fun now." Bristol laughed. "Her husband is a former champion bull rider."

"Like Rhett isn't hot as a firecracker. And my brothers were a pain in my ass when I was growing up. I mean, I got into trouble. But so many guys I liked were afraid to come near me."

"You could bring your son," Bristol suggested to Wynona. "It's not a twenty-one and over party."

"Thank you," Wy said softly. "I'm not sure. He's very moody. In fact, he can be a pain in my ass these days."

Both women laughed and nodded.

"Okay, so what about Thursday? We're doing a book club meeting."

Wynona shrugged again. "I appreciate the invites. But things with Dec are just hard right now."

"All the more reason we need to get you out of your house." Summer poured sweet tea over her ice and took a big drink. "Does he play any sports?"

"He just broke his arm last weekend."

"Oh." Summer nodded. "He was with Patrick Hoffman in that car accident."

"See?" Wynona pointed at Summer. "He wasn't driving, but I'm sure he contributed to the—"

"You haven't met Patrick Hoffman." Summer cut her off with a quick shake of her head.

"Pierce fingered Declan for starting the garage fire the other night," Bristol told Summer.

"They arrested someone for that."

"Mm-hmm." Bristol nodded. "But our very own Pierce

Rooney got a burr up his ass and accused Declan just because he's the new kid in town."

"He's the new kid in town, and he's always in trouble," Wynona mumbled.

"Uh-uh." Bristol shook her head. "Don't let Pierce get away with what he did. Declan's just a kid. Getting in a fight at school is a hell of a lot different than starting fires."

"Pierce is a good guy," Summer said softly. "But he's also a standup community guy. I'm sure he didn't—"

"He apologized," Wy assured her. "It's okay."

Was it, though?

Wynona didn't know. Between her own frustration with Declan, her worry over Declan, her demons still chasing her, and that unwelcome zap of attraction earlier with Pierce, she didn't know her head from her butt right now.

Which only made her wish she could get out for a night with these ladies.

Friends.

Wynona didn't remember the last time she had friends. Anyone she ran around with in Sioux Falls was part of a couple, a couple she and Zach were friends with. And all of them turned their heads whenever things got out of hand between her and Zach. Most likely, they didn't know how bad things could get. And yet, there was a sliver of Wy's heart that blamed those friends for not seeing how badly she needed to be saved.

Or even just supported. Because even with that bitterness inside her, that wish that someone would have recognized what was happening, Wy knew that she wouldn't have allowed it. She would have denied any accusation against Zach.

Downplayed their fights. The gaslighting. As much as she wished she would have had support then, Wynona was the only one who could end it.

She'd had to save herself.

"So, bring him to the book club meeting. Have him bring homework to do."

Wynona laughed at Summer's suggestion.

"I'm serious." Summer shrugged. "If he hates it, maybe he'll think twice before he does something he knows he shouldn't next time."

"Where do you meet?"

"This one's at my house. Gimme your number, and I'll text you."

Wynona handed her phone over to Summer and watched her type in her contact information. When she handed the phone back and pulled her own from her pocket, Wynona rattled off her number.

The tension in her shoulders eased a bit as she finished her tea. She pulled her wallet from her purse and plucked cash out to cover her lunch.

"Thank you, ladies." She nodded. "You have no idea how much I needed this."

thirteen

. . .

WY

She held her breath for the entire five-minute drive to the Skeleton Bar. Sure felt like it anyway, especially when she arrived, put her car in park, and killed the ignition. The way she gasped out loud at what she had done, the overbearing silence in the car—Wynona had to sit for a moment and breathe before getting out.

Declan had asked to go to a friend's house for Halloween. Wynona had been ready to say no, but the friend's mom had called and talked to her. Even then, even knowing Jackson's parents would be home all night and there would be two other boys there—Wy was pretty sure she had heard Declan say they were lame—she had been hesitant to agree to it. But Jackson's dad had volunteered to pick Dec up and bring him home at ten. Wy told herself she had given in because it might have made waves for Dec if she had said no, especially after the generous offer to pick him up. But she was afraid she had made the decision based on her own wants and needs.

She had never seen the parking lot this full. Then again, a Halloween party would draw more guests than a regular Monday afternoon. Still, she couldn't help the shiver of excitement that rolled up her spine as she swung her car door closed and hunched her shoulders deeper in her jacket. Two days ago—even yesterday—she would have sworn the kids would have a warmish night for trick-or-treating. But the air tonight was damp and chilly; a slight breeze teased the curls on her shoulders.

Someone dressed as a spooky butler or maybe Frankenstein opened the door for her as she neared the building. Hard to tell in the dim outdoor lighting, but maybe his skin was green. He simply gave her a nod and held his arm out, gesturing for her to go inside. Wynona felt a goofy smile on her face when she stepped into a pretty good-sized crowd and heard "Thriller" playing. People were crowded around the bar, two or three deep, making her think back to the days when she and Zach had gone to bars together to drink and dance. And then go home and do the things that led to Declan.

Determined to relax and enjoy herself tonight, even if she simply sat at the bar and people watched, Wy gave herself a mental shake. Every table in her line of sight was occupied, but she didn't necessarily want a table. Sitting by herself at a table would really make her feel alone. She edged around a group of guys and made her way to the far end of the bar. To her left was another fairly big seating area with floor to ceiling windows. She hadn't paid much attention to this side of the bar when she had been here in the daytime. Deciding it was probably a beautiful view, she made a mental note to check it out the next time she came for lunch.

The next time?

Realizing she had just made plans for herself, she turned back to the bar with a smile on her face. And found herself staring at Pierce. Dressed as a ghostbuster, complete with a proton pack.

“Hi.”

“Wow.” She laughed as she took him in. Pierce backed up a step so she could see the whole nine yards, including his boots. “You got a ghost in that proton pack?”

“I don’t. Not yet.” He shrugged. “What can I get you?”

“Um.” Since she had only been to the Skeleton Bar for lunch, she had no idea what to order. “I don’t know.”

“Are you a whiskey drinker?”

“No.”

“We’ll work on that,” he said with a small smile. “Cocktail? Beer?”

Because she was driving, whatever Wy ordered, she planned to sip on.

“Vodka cranberry?”

“You bet.”

She watched him as he mixed her drink, though she was aware of the crowd around her. The loud buzz of conversation and laughter nearly drowned out the music on this end of the bar. Pierce delivered her drink back to her, told her he would be back in a minute, and disappeared down the bar to get another drink. Wynona looked around and noted two mermaids, a clown, a vampire, and Cleopatra.

“You made it!” Cleopatra hurried to her and gave her a quick hug. Wynona snorted when she realized it was Bristol under the black wig and makeup.

“I did.”

"Where's Declan?" Bristol looked around. "Did you bring him?"

"No. He went to a friend's house. Tom Bradshaw picked him up."

"Mmm." Bristol nodded. "So, he's friends with Jackson."

Wy wasn't sure if Declan truly considered Jackson a friend or if he was just that desperate to do something tonight. Said a lot about her as a mother that she hadn't cared enough to demand the truth, that she had been that desperate to do something, too.

"Hey, this is my fiancé. Rhett Bailey." Bristol reached back and grabbed on to the guy behind her. Dressed as a roman warrior, the guy turned his attention to Wynona and offered her a big smile. Marc Antony, Wy guessed. "Rhett, this is Wynona Herzog."

"Hey." Rhett reached to shake her hand. "How're you liking Kentucky?"

"It's good." She nodded, because even though it wasn't always good, it was better than Sioux Falls and Zach. "Love the costumes."

Rhett rolled his eyes, but Bristol laughed.

"Summer's husband is Rhett's brother," she told Wynona.

"Oh." Wy sipped her drink. "That's neat."

"What's better?" Rhett snorted.

"Stop it." Bristol slapped her hand gently over his chest.

"My sister is married to Bristol's ex-boyfriend."

Wynona snapped her gaze back to Bristol, certain Rhett was bullshitting her.

“Yeah.” She nodded. “It’s a small town.”

Rhett laughed and leaned closer to drop a kiss on Bristol’s head.

“Careful.” She tried to pull away. “Don’t go pullin’ my wig off again.”

“Mmm.” He grinned and waggled his eyebrows. “I wouldn’t mind doing that again.”

Wynona gaped at her new friend over her glass. Bristol’s face flushed a deep pink, telling Wy exactly what had happened the first time Rhett had pulled her wig off.

“I’m gonna go spell Pierce for a few,” she told Rhett. “You need anything?”

“No, thank you.” Wynona shook her head as Bristol stepped behind the bar.

“My brother did some stripping a couple of years ago,” Rhett grumbled as he tugged at his rather skimpy costume. “I don’t know how he could stand it.”

Wynona blinked at him and slowly lowered her glass to the bar. “I’m sorry. What?”

He laughed. “You’ve been to Kissing Springs, right?”

“I have.”

“Been to the male revue?”

“No. I wasn’t aware there was a male revue.” Wynona laughed. Still worried about Declan, praying he was behaving himself, she had to admit she was glad she had come to the Skeleton Bar tonight. “Your brother is part of the show?”

“No, he just did a few parties. He was a stripping Santa.”

Rhett sipped his amber-colored cocktail. "That's how he and Summer met."

Wynona opened her mouth to answer him, but she had no idea what to say.

"I'll let her tell the story," he said with a genuine smile. "And don't be afraid to ask. Everybody in town knows."

"So, this is the same brother who was a champion bull rider?"

"The very same."

"Hmm." Wy arched her brows and nodded. "So how did you and Bristol meet?"

Rhett chuckled and leaned into the bar. "My brother lives in Kissing Springs. He came up here one night not long after they hooked up. Supposedly to get my dad a specific bottle of whiskey. He just wanted to see Summer again."

"I love it."

"I tagged along so he wouldn't look like the obvious loser that he was." Rhett's smile stretched into a wicked grin. "Bristol was tending bar that night. We hit it off instantly."

"So you've been together for a long time, too."

"Nah. She friend zoned me immediately. Took me a while to get her to notice me."

"Maybe you should have taken your clothes off."

He dropped his head back and laughed. "Don't," he said with a shiver. "I do not want to think about Taj stripping down to a little cock sock."

Pierce appeared at the end of the bar again.

"Why did I just hear the words *cock sock* come out of your mouth?" He leered at Rhett. "Joining the revue?"

"Hell, no." Rhett rolled his eyes. "Talking about Taj."

Pierce glanced at Wynona. "Do you know Taj?"

"No."

"That man's got moves," Pierce reminded Rhett. "He hooked Summer with one shake—"

"Is that Rye Gallaher over there?" Rhett interrupted him. He pointed somewhere over Wynona's shoulder. Pierce laughed and slapped him on the back as he straightened. "It was nice to meet you, Wynona."

"You, too." She nodded as he walked away. The fun, relaxed feeling vanished almost instantly when she found herself staring at Pierce again.

"I get a little break." He tapped his fingers on the bar. "Wanna take a quick walk around? I can show you the campus."

Wynona swallowed hard and glanced at her drink.

"You can take it with you."

Anticipation buzzed through her veins like angry bees. She wasn't afraid of him. Hell, even with the way Zach swung his fists, she hadn't always been afraid of him. She'd just swung hers right back. No, Wynona was a little nervous about stepping outside with Pierce Rooney.

But not because she was afraid he would hurt her.

fourteen

. . .

PIERCE

He led her outside, to the back of the bar, to show her the newest project the Locklands had taken on. The amphitheater was nearly finished; Pierce was looking forward to the first concert they would host. Older, classic country star Wayne Shailey was scheduled for an appearance next spring to kick off a whole new era at Lockland Distilling.

"Wow." Wynona nodded. Her soft voice was full of wonder. "This is incredible."

"I think it's pretty neat," he agreed as he shifted to lean on the wooden railing around the patio. The outdoor amphitheater spread out before them, seating for two thousand fans and a large stage.

"I had no idea there was something like this in this little town."

Pierce glanced at her with a smile. "This and more," he said quietly. "A lot of people think Rodey's a dead end. There's a lot happening if you know where to look."

"You've lived here all your life?"

"Other than the brief stent in Lexington. And college," he answered with a shrug. "I love to travel. But this is home."

"I was born in Iowa. My family moved to South Dakota when I was ten. Met…" She cleared her throat and looked away, suddenly very interested in the long, wooden benches in the amphitheater. "My ex-husband…there. In school."

"College?"

She nodded. "Community college."

"How long were you married?"

Pierce peeked at her again, but deciding she might be more comfortable talking if he wasn't watching her, he looked back at the stage.

"Fifteen years."

"Mmm."

Declan was fifteen, if he remembered right.

"We didn't have to get married," she mumbled. "I mean…"

"You don't have to tell me." He shook his head.

He didn't want Wynona to be uncomfortable, but he found himself holding his breath. Hoping she would keep talking. Her wanted to know more about her.

"We got engaged, and I got pregnant like the next day." Her bitter laugh chilled him. "Maybe that night."

"Did you finish school?"

"Zach went to work in a factory. Which he probably would have anyway. He wasn't interested in an office job."

When Pierce looked her way again, she had her head turned away from him. He couldn't be certain if something had caught her eye, or if she simply didn't want to look at him while she talked.

"I went to school part time and finished my degree."

"What do you do?"

"IT support for banks," she answered. "Well, I work for J. Starr Logistics. Banking software."

"So you work remote?"

"Most of the time." She nodded. "Now and then, I need to be onsite." She swung her gaze back around to meet his eyes. "Software updates."

He chuckled. "They pretty much blow everyone's minds."

"They sure do."

"C'mon." He nodded for her to follow him. "Are you cold?" he asked when he saw her jam her hands in her coat pockets.

"Not bad."

"Want my coat?" he offered, ready to shrug the leather bomber jacket off and hand it over to her.

"No. Thank you."

He nodded. "Do you know much about whiskey? The distilling process?"

"No." She arched her eyebrows at him. "I think my whiskey experience centers around tried some at a party when I was sixteen or seventeen and puked my guts out."

Pierce laughed, but Wynona kept talking.

"Sorry for the visual."

"Happens that way a lot," he told her. "I hear that story often."

"I suppose you're different?"

"Grew up in bourbon country," he mumbled. "I know how to drink it. Which isn't to say I haven't been sick on it a time or two."

They shared a grin.

"You should come in some day for a tour," he suggested.

"Are you a tour guide?"

"No." He shook his head. "I mean, I could do it in a pinch. We're all kind of…cross trained. I'll never be a master distiller, but I could probably wear any other hat here."

"Is your family in the industry?"

"Dad was in agriculture. Farm supply management. Mom teaches fourth grade."

"Interesting."

"Not if you don't like history or math."

Wynona laughed softly.

"Those buildings there?" He pointed as he led her across the campus to the visitors' center and retail shop. Wynona followed the direction of his point and nodded. "Those are rickhouses."

"They look like warehouses."

He shrugged.

"Yeah. Just built on ricks. They're specific to the bourbon industry."

"Are they full?"

"We have ten rick houses here on the campus. Each holds ten thousand barrels."

"Jesus."

"A standard barrel can hold between two hundred and two hundred and fifty bottles."

"Makes sense," she mumbled as she looked around again. "I just never gave it a thought. The actual industry, ya know?"

"It's pretty cool," he told her.

"Big money."

He nodded. "Yeah. It's a huge industry. There's a big bourbon craze going on these days. For a long time, people were more into clear spirits like vodka and gin. Word in the industry is either people lost their minds, or back in the sixties or seventies, young people wanted to rebel against culture. Parents. And do the opposite of what their parents did."

"Damned rebellious kids." She laughed softly.

Despite the laughter—forced laughter, if he read her right—she looked sad. Tired. Overcome with guilt, compassion, Pierce stopped walking and turned to her.

"I'm sorry, Wynona. For the way I came at you at the garage fire."

To his surprise, she locked eyes with him and finally nodded. "Truthfully, Pierce." She sighed and shook her head. "Yeah, it pissed me off. But…I don't know what to do with him."

Her eyes a bit glassy, she nibbled on her lower lip. Pierce fought the urge to touch her, to reach for her hand or brush her hair from her face. She might consider it forward, uninvited. Probably not a good idea to tell her she was pretty, either. Not now.

"Is it the divorce?" he asked quietly. "Did he want to stay with his dad?"

This time, the laughter was tiny, no more than a hiccup that almost sounded like a sob. She ducked her head for a moment, so Pierce waited patiently for her to collect herself.

"No." She sniffled. "No. This behavior started years ago. And, no. I don't think Declan wanted to stay with Zach."

As many questions as he had, Pierce again chose to wait her out. Poking into her business was rude, even if he had warned her yesterday that he would do it. She was clearly hurting. He wanted to know why, if it was Declan or her ex, but he wouldn't push her to say more.

"How about we go back in?" he suggested. "I'll refresh your drink. Are you hungry?"

"I don't need another drink." She shook her head.

"Okay. But are you hungry? We have some good soups on the party menu."

He felt a pang of guilt when she swallowed hard and lifted a hand to dab at her eyes.

"I am hungry."

"Perfect. I'd recommend the chili, but the potato soup is pretty good, too."

She flashed him a smile as they turned to go back toward the bar.

"Thank you."

He held his tongue until they reached the door. But he had to say something before they rejoined the party.

"Wynona?"

“Hmm?” She tipped her head up and looked at him in askance.

“Bristol. Summer. Sheridan. Marlowe.” He shrugged. “They’re good people. I mean…I’m here. You know. If you need to talk. But the girls here…they’re all like family.”

She nodded. Pierce’s eyes were drawn to her throat. He forced himself to look away when he saw her struggling to keep her emotions in check.

“Thanks.”

fifteen

. . .

WY

"No, no, wait!" Sheridan Kennedy leaned into Wynona, giggling as she held her phone out for Wynona to see the screen. "How about this one?"

Wynona laughed at the filter Sheridan had put on her brother Taj's face. Summer, sitting across the small table from them, wore a big smile, but she paid more attention to the baby in her arms than her sister-in-law.

"I'm still trying to wrap my brain around Taj being a sexy Santa stripper," Wynona said as she shook her head.

"Please don't." Sheridan shuddered. "Do you know how scarring it is to think about your brother stripping? Like…for actual women? To think that one liked what she saw enough to leave with him that night?"

Summer snickered and reached for her coffee.

Wynona looked around the little coffee shop. True to form with the rest of the world, French Kiss Coffee seemed to think the passing of Halloween meant it was now the Christmas season. A song talking about, probably called "Christmas Dreamin'" played softly in the background. There was no tree up yet, but Wynona could imagine it.

She didn't mind, actually. Bristol had called her Thursday afternoon to invite her to get coffee with the girls today. Wynona had almost said no. She wasn't thrilled about leaving Declan home alone. But if there was a time to do it, an early Saturday morning was it. Declan had been sleeping when she left the house earlier.

Talking to Pierce on Halloween night had changed something inside her. Kind of broken the dam, maybe. She wasn't ready to offer a PowerPoint on her sucky life and the stupid decisions she had made to date. But the idea of making friends, of having people to hang out with again, had been so tempting.

"He still dances for me," Summer told them now.

Sheridan covered her mouth and shook again like she had the willies. The rest of them laughed, Wynona included. She had yet to meet Taj, but she figured from the stories she had heard that she would like him.

"Rhett—"

"No." Sheridan lunged over the table and grabbed Bristol's hand. "If you do, I'll start talking about Trey, and that could get super weird, super-fast."

Wynona waited, her stomach in knots, wondering if the comment would cause the mood to shift at the table. But Bristol only laughed.

"Does he still sleep all curled up in the fetal position?"

"He does." Sheridan nodded.

"Okay, that's weird," Marlowe mumbled.

Wynona glanced at the slender, dark-haired woman. Apparently, she had some long-distance guy she talked to sometimes. Bristol had filled her in on that first thing this morning, since they were the first two here. Marlowe had a kid at home, but that guy wasn't in the picture. She hadn't dated much after her son was born. But she had gotten a little flirty and exchanged kisses with some guy who had crossed her path last year. According to Bristol, they still talked and texted, but Marlowe didn't think anything would ever come of it.

Wynona wondered if Pierce knew about the long-distance thing. He had talked a bit about Marlowe, but he'd never said much.

"Are the girls excited about Santa coming?" Bristol asked Summer. After a beat of silence, they all broke into laughter, Summer included, even though her face was a bright Christmas red.

"Ohmygod." Sheridan groaned and stood up. "On that note, I gotta pee."

Wynona watched her walk to the back of the building and disappear into the ladies' room.

"Yes." Summer cleared her throat. "They are very excited for Christmas. Although, Stella asked for a horse again."

"She still carry Rosie around with her everywhere she goes?" Marlowe asked. "Stick horse," she explained to Wynona.

"Everywhere but Marley and Gil's." Summer sighed. "Marley won't allow it."

"That woman's got a stick up her butt," Bristol mumbled.

"She's okay," Summer argued.

"No, she's not. You just have to play nice as the stepmom."

Summer shrugged and patted Beckett's back. The baby was asleep on her shoulder.

"Is your ex remarried?" Summer asked Wynona.

Wynona stared at her blankly for a moment. "I don't think so." She laughed and shrugged. "We don't have a lot to do with each other."

"Except Declan?" Summer prodded.

Wynona winced. "It's…complicated. We talk when we need to about Dec."

"He doesn't want to see him?"

Wynona wasn't sure if Summer was asking if Zach didn't want to see Declan or the other way around.

"They don't have much of a relationship," she hedged. "But then again, I'm not sure Declan and I have much of a relationship."

"Is he angry?" Marlowe reached for her cup, drawing Wynona's gaze to the tattoos that started on the back of her hand and disappeared under the sleeve of her black sweater.

"Yeah." Wynona nodded. "You could say that."

"Way asked me about his dad last summer." Marlowe took a deep breath. She directed her intense stare at Wynona. "He asked a lot when he was in kindergarten. But then he dropped it. I never know how to answer him."

Sheridan joined them again.

"Zach and I both made some big mistakes," Wynona said quietly. "Unfortunately, Dec's just modeling the behavior he's learned from us."

She felt Bristol watching her closely now.

"Fighting," Bristol guessed.

"Mmm."

"Wait." Summer leaned forward, but it was Sheridan who spoke next.

"Your ex was abusive?"

Wynona cleared her throat. "Kind of."

"There's no kind of." Summer shook her head. "Did he hurt you?"

Wynona sucked in a deep breath and swallowed hard. "Yeah. But I had a short fuse. I learned to fight back."

"Good for you." Marlowe nodded.

"Not for our son," Wynona said softly.

"It's not your fault," Bristol told her.

"Isn't it?"

"You were defending yourself."

Wynona glanced at Sheridan. "I modeled violence as a way to handle violence."

"What were you supposed to do?" Summer asked. "Take it? What would that have taught Declan?"

"I should have left."

"You did."

"Sooner," Wynona argued. "I should have left a long time ago. I think Declan is angry with his dad for using his fists. And ashamed of me for letting it happen as long as I did."

"You can't beat yourself up about that," Sheridan told her. "You left. You're trying to do the right thing now."

"The right thing," Wynona repeated. "Dragging my fifteen-year-old son across the country so he can start fights at school. Blaze a trail of bad behavior so everyone thinks the worst of him."

"I think Pierce feels horrible about that."

"What did Pierce do?" Marlowe glanced from Wynona to Bristol.

"Accused Declan of starting that garage fire."

"Mmm." Marlowe flinched. "He cares. Too much. About everyone."

"He does," Bristol agrees.

"I think he was maybe just upset about Amy Church's kid."

Wynona jerked her gaze from her cup to Marlowe. "What?"

"Pierce and Amy dated. They were tight. Still good friends."

That explained a lot.

Wynona sighed and shrugged. "He apologized. But I have to admit…"

"What?"

Summer passed the baby to Bristol. "Take him for a sec."

Wynona watched Summer head back toward the bathroom.

"If Dec hadn't been with me all that day, I might have thought the same thing."

"Has he played with fire before?" Marlowe asked her. "Because I'm not sure every rebellious kid is just gonna start setting fires. That's a whole different level of dangerous behavior."

Wynona sat back and gave Marlowe's comment some thought.

"You're right." She nodded. "He's never done things to be hateful or vicious. Well." She laughed humorlessly. "Other than the way he talks to me. But…"

"But what?" Sheridan coaxed her to keep talking.

"What if it gave him the idea?"

"Did you tell him? What Pierce said to you?" Bristol looked shocked.

"No." Wynona frowned. "Of course not. But there were rumors at school the next day that Dec had something to do with it."

"Do you think someone overheard Pierce talking to you at the fire?"

"I don't know." Wynona gave herself a mental shake. "Someone change the subject! Quick. I don't wanna talk about Declan anymore."

"Let's talk about Thanksgiving," Sheridan suggested.

sixteen

. . .

PIERCE

Mav tipped his pint glass up in a greeting as Pierce made his way from the door to the bar. Marlowe pulled a beer and slid the glass over to Pierce as he sat down. He looked around the Iron Stag as he took a long drink, finally put the glass down on the bar, and met Mav's eyes. He liked the Stag, and he always enjoyed hanging around to catch up with Marlowe, but Pierce found himself wishing for prettier scenery at the moment.

A brunette with loose waves over her shoulders. Dark eyes. Pretty smile, although most times, she was stingy with it, hesitant to share it. Then again, that made it all the more appealing to Pierce.

He liked her.

Wynona Herzog. The mother of the kid he had accused of arson.

Part of him still felt a little guilty for that. Wynona hadn't said much to him about her past, about Declan. But it was obvious she was worried about her son. Maybe it had been unfair of

Pierce to go at her like that at the scene of the garage fire, to suggest her kid had something to do with it.

Then again, Pierce loved the Rodey community. It was that love of community and neighbor, as well as the awe of the flames, the unpredictable power of fire, that had driven him to become a volunteer firefighter. He took his position seriously, and he went out of his way to help people. He always had. And after the bullshit shenanigans the new kid had pulled just before the day of the fire, it was a logical assumption to think he might be involved. As bad as that made Pierce feel, he still believed he was justified in his suspicions.

Hard to get to know Wynona better, though, if he was going to look at her son that way all the time.

"What?" Mav's voice finally pulled him from his thoughts.

"Hmm?"

"You're looking at me like I'm the turkey at Thanksgiving dinner, and you haven't had a meal for weeks."

Pierce snorted and rolled his eyes.

"I see you're still full of shit."

Mav flashed his trademark grin. His family owned a ranch; that grin and his blue eyes and probably something about his work-won muscles and his daddy's money had scored Maverick damned near every woman in town and the surrounding area.

"Makes life more fun."

Pierce glanced at Marlowe as she sidled up to the service side of the bar again.

"Want something to eat?" she asked him.

He probably shouldn't. There was no reason Pierce couldn't go home and fix himself something to eat. But he found himself nodding in response, and he knew there would be a burger and fries in front of him within fifteen minutes.

"Hear you been nosing around the new girl," Mav announced.

Mav was a true cowboy. He dressed the part, but his boots were old and scuffed and his jeans worn and faded. When he worked, he wore a hat, but often, when he came into the bar, he'd leave the hat in his truck. If Pierce were into guys, he might wonder how the hell Mav could wear a damned cowboy hat for hours and not have hat head when he chucked the hat to come into the Stag.

Pierce sighed and shook his head, eyes on the back bar. He took a moment to control his response, just in case Mav was asking because he was interested. No way in hell he was going to let Maverick Pressey take a crack at Wynona. She probably wasn't ready for anything with anyone, Pierce included. And while he didn't hate the idea of getting to know her better, of claiming her as his, he wouldn't push her. But Mav didn't need to know that. On the other hand, Pierce couldn't go spouting off to his buddy that Wynona was his and therefore Mav should keep his distance. What the hell would Wynona say about that if word got back to her?

"We've talked," he finally answered.

"She's pretty." Maverick tipped his glass up for another swallow.

"I don't think she's your type." Pierce shrugged. "She's got a kid. She doesn't get out much."

"Maybe all the more reason to introduce myself to her." Mav

cocked his head at Pierce and quirked an eyebrow. "Get her mind off…things."

Pierce held his breath for a moment. But before he could say a word, Mav barked a laugh and dropped a heavy hand on his shoulder.

"Man, I'm just bullshittin' you," he promised. "I've heard a few people say you're into her."

"What?" Pierce stopped his hand enroute to his mouth, glad he hadn't taken a drink yet. He would be choking now, whacking at his chest to swallow.

"Bristol says you've got a thing for her."

Bristol would know. Pierce stared at Mav for a second and finally shrugged. If anyone knew what Pierce was thinking, it was Bristol and Marlowe. Bristol read people like Marlowe read all those damned romantasy books she had tattooed all over her arms. And he and Marlowe were close enough that she could almost read his mind.

"Maybe."

"Bristol also says she thinks new girl's got eyes for you."

"Now, that I know is bullshit," Pierce argued.

Mav glanced over Pierce's shoulder and sat upright suddenly, his face broadcasting his surprise. Wondering if Wynona had just come inside the Iron Stag, Pierce swung his gaze back toward the door to see his little sister looking around cautiously, as if she was uncertain about coming inside.

"What the hell?" Pierce mumbled as he slid off the stool. Mav locked eyes with him, that damned snide grin gone, replaced by the worry Pierce felt. He shrugged at his buddy as he turned to the door and stepped closer to his sister. "Lyndi?"

She whooshed out a big sigh when their eyes met, like she was relieved to see him. Pierce eyed her carefully as he made his way to where she stood. She wore a long winter coat, but from what he could see, she was tiny underneath it. Like she'd lost weight she didn't have to lose.

"Hey." She flashed a smile and leaned into him when he hugged her.

"What are you doing here?"

"Just." She shook her head as she stepped back. "Needed to come home for a while. Are you busy?"

Slinging his arm over her shoulders, he coaxed her out of the doorway where she still stood. "No. Let me buy you a beer. And a cheeseburger." He looked at her again, this time obvious with the once over. "Or two."

seventeen

. . .

PIERCE

Mav chatted Lyndi up for a few minutes, but he left them alone when Pierce suggested to his sister that they grab a table. Marlowe understood the assignment without Pierce saying a word to her. Within minutes of grabbing a two-top a good distance from the bar, she delivered two plates to them. One was loaded down with a cheeseburger and fries. The other was an impossible burger. It was one thing for the Locklands to start serving vegan options; the Skeleton Bar was a trendy, upscale bourbon bar. But Pierce had rolled his eyes when James and Elaine Murray, the owners of the Iron Stag, put a few vegetarian and vegan items on their menu. After all, the Iron Stag was a plain old, middle-of-nowhere tavern.

Now he appreciated it. When Lyndi left town, she had been a vegan. It had been years, but from the looks of it, she still preferred twigs and grass to meat.

"Thank you." She stared at him for a moment with doe eyes, making him feel guilty for his thoughts. Hell, he didn't care if his sister thought it was wrong or gross to eat meat. He just wanted her to be happy.

And healthy.

"What's going on?" he asked with a curt nod. He lifted his own burger and took a big bite. He didn't have much of an appetite now, not after seeing just how little, how thin his sister had become. But maybe if he paid more attention to his food than her, she would talk to him. Confide in him.

From the corner of his eye, he watched her stare at her plate for a moment and finally slide her coat off. He snuck a peek at her when she turned in her chair to lay the coat over it. She still didn't say anything, but Pierce sighed softly, relieved when she picked up her burger for a bite.

"Home for Thanksgiving," she answered.

"A month early." He tipped his head at her when she finally looked at him.

"I quit my job." She spoke softly once she swallowed the food in her mouth.

"Dad said you were thinking about it." He watched her dab her napkin over her mouth and then reach for the beer Marlowe had pulled for her.

"I think I want to move back."

As curious as he was about what was driving his sister back to little old Rodey, Kentucky, Pierce only nodded and sat back in his chair. No need to jump down her throat about it.

"Hmm." He glanced at the bar where Mav was still talking to Marlowe. If it were anyone other than Marlowe, Pierce would wonder if she needed a rescue. But Marlowe didn't take shit from anyone, and she had never been into Mav as anything other than a friend.

"Mom said they're thinking about moving to Florida."

Lyndi's urgent tone turned his attention back to her.

"Dad mentioned it."

"So. My boss." She cleared her throat. "Was a total jerk—"

"Did he—? What did he do to you?"

"No, no, no." Lyndi shook her head. "No. Not like that. I mean, I think he's a dick with his wife, but nothing like that. Sales have been down, and everything has suddenly become my fault. If I did this better or didn't do that…."

"He's gaslighting you."

"Kind of." She nodded. "He's been aggressive with other employees."

"Aggressive?"

"Got in this guy's face the other day." Lyndi sighed and picked up her burger again. "I gave him my notice, and those last two weeks were hell."

Pierce flinched. "Good for you for sticking it out, but also, why the hell didn't you just tell him to go to hell and leave?"

She chuckled.

"Okay." He grabbed a few fries and munched for a few moments. "So, what the hell was going on with the girls harassing you at the library?"

"Mmm." Lyndi rested her elbow on the table and propped her chin in her hand. "I went out with this guy a few times. I don't know if one of them was an ex or if one of them just had a thing for him. But they followed me everywhere for a few days. Keyed my car. Threw shit in my yard. I had to be careful about when I let Linus outside."

"Who's Linus?"

"My dog."

"You have a—" Pierce shook his head. "Where is he now?"

"Mom and Dad's."

"You've already been to Mom and Dad's? When did you get in?"

"Last night."

"And you didn't call me?"

"It was late, Pierce. And I slept late today. And you were working."

"Is that all, Lyndi?"

"What?" She pushed her plate away, over half the burger gone by now. "What do you mean? Are you mad at me for not—"

"No." He waved her question away and reached for his beer. "Is that really all that's going on?"

She stared at him silently.

"Let me rephrase." He smiled, hoping she understood that he wasn't being a jerk. "I'm glad you're here. It's just that you were hell bent on getting out of here. A hundred percent sure Rodey wasn't the place for you."

The look on her face, the knowing smile, made him squirm.

"That was a few years ago," she reminded him. "I loved it for a while. I did…things." She stopped here and flashed a big grin, one that made him hope to hell she didn't plan to confide those things in him. "It was fun. But I'm bored."

"And Rodey is going to provide entertainment for you, how?"

"Maybe bored's not the right word."

"Don't even tell me you're homesick."

She laughed softly. "Not exactly. But, I'm over the itch that made me pack my bags and run. I'm not saying I'll stay here. But maybe something closer to home."

"Kissing Springs?"

She shrugged. "Maybe. Maybe Louisville. Lexington. I don't know. I think I'm just ready to reinvent myself."

Pierce finished his beer, wiped the back of his hand over his mouth, and nodded. "Okay. I get that. I'm sure Mom's thrilled that you're back."

"She is." Lyndi nodded. "I think the holidays will be fun."

"They will," he agreed.

"Can you get me on at Lockland?"

"I can put in a good word for you, but I'm sure you don't need it."

"I mean, lots of distilleries here. But do I wanna compete with you?"

"It's a friendly competition," he answered with a small smile.

Lyndi swept her gaze around the bar, studied the faces at the tables near them, and finally looked back at him.

"Just do not ask me to hook you up with Mav Pressey."

Lyndi cleared her throat and shook her head. Pierce groaned when she wouldn't meet his eyes.

"Jesus, Lyndi. How old were you?"

"You really wanna talk about it?"

"Nope. I don't." He shuddered. "Ever. Let me give you Summer Lockland's number. Give her a call and tell her you're looking for a job."

"I could just go in—"

Pierce fixed a firm look on her. "You just asked me to hook you up," he reminded her. He didn't need to. If the Locklands needed help, they would hire her. But Pierce liked the idea of his little sister getting to know Summer. And her friends—including Bristol and Marlowe.

"Right." She nodded.

Pierce shared Summer's contract information to her.

"And do not let me catch you around Pressey." He snagged his empty beer glass and pointed at hers. "You want another?"

"Sure."

eighteen

. . .

WY

"Look. You tried it."

Wynona dropped her head back and took a deep breath. Eyes closed, she waited for Zach to continue. No point in interrupting his lecture, because then it would turn into an ugly, angry rant. She didn't like either, but the ugly, angry rant would send her back to days she would rather forget.

"And you obviously can't handle him." The arrogance in his tone pissed her off more than what he was actually saying. "I mean, damn, Wy, the kid's been in trouble since you got there. Wouldn't surprise me a damned bit if he did start that fire you told me about."

Damned if she knew why she had shared that tidbit with Zach.

"Send him back to me, and I'll whip him into shape."

The words chased a chill up her spine. To her knowledge, Zach had never taken a fist or even his open palm to her son. But again, his words created a hell of an image in her mind.

And even if he didn't lay a hand on Zach, if he somehow laid down the law and that was enough to keep Declan in line, Wynona still worried he would teach the kid things she didn't want him to learn.

Like how to hate women.

She would say how to meet violence with violence, but then, she'd already messed that up. But since moving, since leaving Zach and Sioux Falls behind, she had been calm. She hadn't laid a hand on Declan; that would never change. But she didn't have Zach around, ripping on her every move, gaslighting her. She didn't have much of anything in her life making her want to throw hands the way she had done with her ex-husband.

Well, nothing other than Declan.

He was watching her when she opened her eyes. Sitting at the kitchen table, biology book open on the table in front of him, Declan was clearly more interested in her phone call with his dad than he was his homework. The quiet days had ended today with another phone call, this one from the tiny little market in Rodey—barely big enough to change your mind once inside. Declan had been caught shoplifting.

Bad enough.

What had infuriated Wy was that he had stolen a pack of gum. He didn't chew gum. Never had. Obviously, Declan had done it simply because it was wrong. Maybe because he would be caught. Because he knew it would cause trouble for her.

"I'm not sending him back to Sioux Falls," she said quietly. Was it her imagination, or did Dec's shoulders slump? Was he relieved? Disappointed? Did he want to go back and live with Zach? What would she do if that were the case?

"Well, then, you better figure out how to control him. He's gonna be in prison before he's out of high school with how you've raised him."

Wynona felt the anger burning under her skin. If she were the old Wynona, if she still lived with Zach, that comment would have driven her to strike at him. He would have laughed, only fueling her anger.

"He's a lot like you," she told her ex.

"Right. Blame it on me." Zach did that damned sarcastic laugh again. "Tell ya what, hon. You don't get him on the straight and narrow, I'll be down there to collect him next time you call me."

"Well, then I guess I won't be calling you anymore, Zach." She hung up before he could respond and turned her phone off immediately.

"He wants me to live with him?" Declan asked.

Wynona bit off her reply, took a moment to breathe rather than snap at him.

"Do you want to live with your dad, Dec?" She lowered herself slowly to sit at the table with him. The dinner dishes were put away, the kitchen clean. Wy had only called Zach to share the latest because she felt like it was his right to know what was going on. No more of that. If he wanted to find out, he could either call his son or drive down here and see.

Not that she would give up without a fight if he did show up here tomorrow.

"No." He shrugged and looked back at this open textbook. Wynona studied the top of his head, his thick dirty-blond hair. She would swear his shoulders were getting wider, thicker with muscle. He wore an old Pink Floyd t-shirt, one she was pretty sure he took from Zach before they left. The notes and signatures on his cast had made her feel good when she first started seeing them, thinking he was fitting in. That he would settle down and like it here. But now she wondered if he had fallen in with the wrong crowd.

Wynona would never claim her kid was innocent of everything, but was it possible he had found the wrong crowd that would egg him on? Push him to escalate the bad behaviors?

"And what if he shows up and demands that you go with him?"

"Can he do that?" Declan tipped his chin up slightly to stare at her with dark eyes. "You're my mom."

"He could take me to court," she said simply. "Make the claim that I'm not a good mom."

"But you are."

"Am I?" She shrugged.

"Your friends would stand up for you."

Maybe they would. The girlfriends she had made here seemed like loyal, giving people. But what about someone like Pierce Rooney? He might like to see Declan yanked away from her, both to save Declan and punish her.

"Tell me this." She sat back in the chair. "If I'm a good mom, why do you do the things you do, Dec?"

"I hate it here."

"Okay, so we move? Is that it?" She tipped her head. "Where do you wanna go? Tell me."

When he didn't say anything, she leaned forward again and

reached over the table to touch his hand. Declan jerked away from her and hid hands in his lap.

"Sioux Falls? You wanna go back there?"

"No." He sighed. "I hate it. Here."

Wynona gasped softly when he tapped his chest.

"Why?" she whispered.

"Why not?" He straightened and met her eyes. "I'm a burden to you. I don't wanna be here."

"Declan." She lunged over the table, but he pulled back to put space between them. "I love you. You know that, right?"

"I do." He nodded. "But I think your life would be easier if I weren't around."

"It wouldn't." She swiped at her eyes. "It wouldn't. Don't you ever, ever think that."

Eyes on his book again, he shrugged in response. His aloof manner might have hurt her, but his glassy eyes ripped her heart out.

"Can you help me study for a test?"

"Absolutely."

nineteen

...

PIERCE

"Hey." He offered Wynona a smile as he dried a glass and put it under the bar. "Haven't seen you around for a while."

"Hey." She sighed as she climbed up to sit on the barstool he had come to think of as hers. Pierce almost reached for another glass to dry, but he hesitated, eyes on her. She looked tired, a little bit pale.

"You okay?" He moseyed down the bar to stand in front of her. Wynona slapped her phone and keys down on the bar and then put her hands on her face. She closed her eyes, drew in a deep breath, held it for a moment, and finally, let it out slowly. Like she was counting to ten.

"Yeah."

The urge to jump in, to hammer her with questions, was stronger than it had been with his little sister the other night. And yet, he knew the best way to coax Wynona into talking if something was bothering her was patience. Giving her plenty of time and space.

"What can I get you?"

"Something strong."

He flinched. "I've got plenty of strong stuff, but you told me you don't like whiskey."

"I'm not interested in what it tastes like." She met his eyes and stared him down.

"You're driving?" He flicked his gaze to her keys.

"Jesus, Pierce, I'm not sixteen, okay?"

He held his hands up in surrender. "Sure, sure. I'll pour you the flagship."

"Thank you."

Her phone vibrated and scooted a bit on the bar as he selected a bottle of Lockland Five Year and a Glencairn glass. From the corner of his eye, he watched her ignore it. When he had poured a finger for her, he set the Glencairn on the bar in front of her.

"It's not a shot."

He spoke calmly, ready for her to take another verbal swing at him. But she only nodded.

"You need something hard and strong, something to shoot, I got that at my place."

Wynona's snort, the amused look on her face, surprised him. He wasn't embarrassed; mostly, he was impressed that even in her current state, her mind had gone *there*. Not at all where he had intended, but if it made her laugh, he was good with it.

He was also a little bit aroused. Not that he would admit that. For fuck's sake. It was just after three on a Thursday afternoon. Nothing like a damned boner in the middle of the afternoon when he was at work.

Her short nails were buffed and natural, but her fingers were long and slender. She wore no rings, no jewelry that he could see. But he couldn't take his eyes off her hands as she lifted the glass to nose the bourbon.

"Wait." He leaned on the bar.

"What? Isn't that what you're supposed to do?"

"Well, yeah." He shrugged when she laughed at him. "But you don't like it."

"I don't, but I have tasted bourbon before, Pierce."

"Where?"

"Few different places."

"With your ex?"

Rather than answer him, she took a small sip of the amber-colored liquid. To her credit, she didn't make a face as she swallowed. But she shuddered as she lowered the glass.

"I don't know what to do," she said softly, obviously upset about something. Before Pierce could say anything, the door opened behind her and Summer led his sister into the bar.

"Hey." Summer grinned at him and then turned her attention to Wynona. "Hey, Wy. This is Lyndi. She's a new hire."

"Really, Summer?" He rolled his eyes.

"What?" She laughed and shrugged dramatically.

"She's *my* sister."

Wynona perked up at the word and turned on the barstool to look closely at Lyndi.

"Lyndi, this is my friend Wynona."

Pierce studied his sister for a moment. Dressed in wide leg jeans, her combat boots weren't quite as noticeable today. She wore a purple sweater; her dark blond hair was pulled back in one of those loose, messy buns that seemed to say there was no time or effort involved in getting ready to leave the house.

"Her friends," Summer shot him a droll look, "call her Wy."

"Hi, Wy." Lyndi shook Wynona's hand. "Nice to meet you."

"Wanna do dinner later?" Summer asked Wynona. Pierce bit his tongue. First, she swooped in and introduced his sister to her, and now she was asking her about dinner?

"I can't." Wynona shook her head.

"Raincheck." Summer touched her arm as she led Lyndi behind the bar and into the kitchen.

"She's pretty."

"You sound surprised." Pierce narrowed his eyes at her. Wynona laughed softly.

"No. Just interesting. All you people down here are pretty to look at."

"You fit right in," he said sincerely. "Trust me."

Wynona arched her brows and ducked her chin as a blush climbed her pale face.

"What's going on?" He leaned on the counter again.

"Nothing."

"Wy."

Her lips curved at his use of her nickname, but the smile faded quickly. She didn't correct him.

"Dec was caught shoplifting Tuesday." She sighed.

"In Rodey? What'd he steal? A loaf of bread from the market?"

"A pack of gum," she answered.

Pierce pressed his lips together and nodded. "Well, to be honest with you, I think that kinda stuff happens a lot around here."

"Don't."

"Don't what?"

"Try to make me feel better."

"It's true. When we were kids, Evie Carter got caught stealing at the Five and Dime store."

"You have a Five and Dime?"

"Not anymore." He shook his head. "That's not the point. It's like a rite of passage around here."

"Says the guy who accused Declan of arson."

Pierce flinched.

"My ex-husband thinks Dec's problems are because I'm a bad mom. He has strongly suggested Dec go back to live with him."

"I'm sorry."

"Part of me thinks he's just messing with me." She licked her lips. "Making me *worry* that he'll just show up here eventually. And part of me thinks he *will* just show up here one of these days."

"Would he hurt you?"

“Oh, he would try,” she answered with a nod. “He would. But I’d hurt him right back.”

Pierce’s hand moved before he realized what he was doing. Together, they watched him stroke his fingers over hers.

“It’s hard to imagine a pretty hand like this taking a swing at someone.”

“I have a pretty mean right hook.” She quirked a brow at him. “Just sayin’.”

“I actually kind of find that attractive,” he confessed with a smile. “Although, you should have never had to resort to that to defend yourself.”

“I don’t care about myself, Pierce,” she whispered. “I worry about Declan.”

twenty

. . .

WY

"Would he hurt Declan?"

Wynona stared at Pierce for a moment, wondering why he cared. Was he just being the stereotypical bartender? She didn't think so, but damned if she could think straight these days.

"No." She shook her head. "I would have left him a long time ago if I thought he would hurt Dec."

Pierce nodded, but he lifted his gaze over her shoulder. Judging from the subtle change in the air pressure behind her, Wynona assumed someone had come inside the bar.

"Excuse me for just a second." Pierce touched her hand again.

She nodded, eyes glued to the glass on the bar as he moved away to help the newcomer. As if she didn't have enough on her mind, now her heart raced from Pierce's touch. She didn't have time to be involved, *to want* to be involved with anyone. And if she did have that time, that inclination, she wouldn't just choose someone like Pierce Rooney. Someone who had pointed the finger of blame at her son.

Then again.

She snorted softly. Cue the ridiculous circular thoughts. Then again, Pierce had apologized. He had seemed concerned about Declan. Then again, Wynona had her own doubts about Declan and his reckless, rebellious behavior. Then again, it had been so long since anyone—

"What's funny?"

"Hmm?" Wynona gave herself a mental shake and looked up to meet Pierce's eyes.

"You have this…" He leaned on the bar again and tipped his head to study her face. "Intriguing…smirk on your face."

She laughed softly. "Just. I just have so much going on in my head. I can't even think straight."

"Might help to talk about it," he suggested.

With a deep breath and a long, slow exhale, Wynona lifted her glass again for another sip. The bourbon wasn't horrible, but it would never be her go-to for a drink on a night out. Part of her was ready to jump on Pierce's offer of something hard and stiff, something to shoot, at his house. And parts of her still tingled with arousal at the double entendre she was sure he didn't mean to make.

"You don't wanna listen to me rant about my ex or my son."

"Try me."

"Why?" Her voice was gruff with emotion, so she took another quick sip to drag the emotion down the hatch.

"Because I like you," he said simply. "And I don't like that you're unhappy."

Not the answer she expected. She'd assumed he would make a crack about smiles and pretty faces. Maybe what he said was just as much a line as what she assumed he would say. But it was the right line. It worked for her anyway.

She laughed and dabbed at her eyes.

"You wouldn't happen to know any therapists or counselors in the area, would you?"

"For Declan."

She nodded.

"I don't. But you could mention it to Summer. If she doesn't know, her parents might. They know everyone in the area. They're discreet."

"It's not like the whole damned town doesn't know who Declan is by now."

Pierce winced at her words. "Let me meet him."

"Why?"

"I don't know. I'll put him to work. Maybe some responsibility would be good for him."

"Maybe so." She shrugged. "But he's in a cast right now."

"Won't be forever." Pierce glanced around the room and reached for the towel he had been using to dry glasses when she came in. "Maybe he just needs a guy around."

"A father figure."

"I didn't say that," he argued with a shake of his head. "I just…think…it might be good for him. And it might be good for you."

"Having you around?" she quirked an eyebrow at him. The second she did it, the second the words were out of her mouth, she blushed. Jesus, she was flirting with him in the same conversation about worrying about her son?

He grinned and shrugged. "Sure, I like that idea. But I meant it would be good for you to have some Wynona time. A spa day. A night out with friends."

"I'm not a spa kind of girl," she argued. "And definitely not when my son's—"

"Okay." Pierce nodded. "Read a book. Curl up on your sofa with a book. Watch a movie. Take a nap."

She blinked at him, thinking he just needed to add the all-of-the-above option. Including having him around more. Coffee with the girls had been great. She would love to do more of that. Each of them had welcomed her with open arms, and Wynona sensed she could ask any of them if she needed something.

But she couldn't ignore the way Pierce Rooney made her feel. The tender smiles he aimed at her. The way he talked to her, but even more so, the way he listened to her.

"Okay."

"Okay?" His grin lit up the bar. "Can I come by your place tonight?"

"To see—"

"Dec, of course." He nodded. "I could bring a pizza over."

"I hate rewarding him after the shoplifting thing."

"That was Tuesday. It's two days later. And you have to eat."

Wynona dropped her head back and laughed softly. "You drive a hard bargain."

“I’m a safe driver, though,” he countered. She held his gaze boldly, wondering if he was telling her he was safe. For her. That he wouldn’t hurt her.

Or was he still talking about Declan?

“Sure.” She nodded and turned her phone over. “Speaking of Declan, I need to go.”

“Okay.”

“He had detention today,” she said with a sharp smile. “Mouthed off to his biology teacher yesterday about a test question.” Never mind that she had helped him study for that test, and he had known the material backwards and forwards.

Pierce acknowledged her comment with a slight nod.

“I gotta pick him up.”

“What’s your phone number?”

She rattled off her phone number, expecting him to write it down.

“Aren’t you going to write it down?”

“I won’t forget,” he promised her. “I’ll text you after five.”

twenty-one

• • •

PIERCE

If Wynona had asked him to drive to Kissing Springs for pizza, he would have. But when he texted her earlier, as he was leaving work, she said it didn't matter to her where he ordered from. The pizza place in Rodey—hell, Pierce had been here most of his life and didn't know the place by any name but Pizza, and some of the letters on the sign were burned out—had decent food pizza and wings. It was cheap enough, too. Just no atmosphere in the tiny place with two tables and grease-covered vinyl seats.

He ignored the doorbell now and tapped on the door itself. While he waited for her to answer, he took a moment to look around the front of the place. He knew the house, though it had been years since he'd been inside. When he was in high school, he knew the family that lived here. Now, as far as he knew, it was a rental. The sandalwood-colored brick hadn't changed, of course, but the landscaping was fresh and tidy. If he remembered right, overgrown hedges had surrounded the front of the house back in the day. Now there were small evergreens on the corners and colorful flowers in front of the house. Pierce didn't know snapdragons from sunflowers, but that didn't mean he couldn't appreciate the look.

When the door opened, he spun around to find Wynona watching him. Dressed in leggings and an oversized sweatshirt, she looked like a high school girl, slumped in the doorway, the hint of a smile on her face.

"The place looks great," he told her with another look around the yard. An old-fashioned lantern lamp near the driveway threw golden light over the well-kept lawn.

"Thanks. I didn't do it."

"But you do the upkeep?"

She shrugged his question off, as if it was no big deal that her yard looked good.

"I water the plants and mow the yard," she answered. "My landlord does the planting and stuff."

"Who is it?"

"Stan Koonz."

"Mm." Pierce nodded. "Nice guy. I brought pizza. And wings."

"Mmm." She tsskd and shook her head. "Shouldn't have brought wings."

"Why? Are you allergic to chicken?" he asked incredulously.

"No." She laughed softly and pushed the screen door open wider for him to step inside. "Dec loves wings. He's supposed to be in trouble."

"Well, imagine how hard it'll be for him to eat them with the cast on one arm."

"Evil." Wynona met Pierce's eyes. "I like it."

"Glad you're not my mom."

Her eyes lit up at his teasing.

"Beer?" she asked as she nodded for him to follow her to the back of the little house.

"Sounds good." He scanned the small living room and smaller kitchen, noting the changes but remembering the good times he'd had here as a kid with his friends. He set the food on the table and took the longneck bottle from her when she handed it to him. "Where's Declan?"

"Upstairs." She swung the door of the refrigerator closed and pulled some paper plates from the small pantry cabinet. Back in the day, that's where the Willers kept the cleaning supplies. He pushed away a memory of a food fight between himself and Jeff Willer and glanced toward the stairs to his left.

"Did he know I was coming?"

"Told him a friend was bringing pizza."

"A friend." Pierce held his bottle out and waited until she lifted hers and tapped them together. "I like the sound of that."

"He's probably gonna be a little jerk, Pierce," she said quietly. "I love that kid to the damned moon and back, but he's probably gonna be horrible tonight."

"Bring it on, Wy." Pierce shook his head. "I can handle it."

Wynona arched her brows as if to remind him she had warned him. He shrugged out of his coat as she moved closer to the stairs to holler at Declan.

"Sit down," she told him when she turned back to the table. Pierce sat after she did, but they both turned their attention to the sound of Declan on the steps. The kid bounded down the last few like he was throwing himself over the finish line after running a grueling marathon. But he pulled up short and froze in place when he saw Pierce sitting with his mom at the table.

"What's going on?" he asked. He turned his attention from Pierce to Wynona.

"This is Pierce Rooney," Wynona told him. "He brought pizza for dinner."

"And what?" Declan looked back at Pierce with a suspicious frown. "Like, are you with the Children's Protective Services or something? Are you gonna take me away from my mom?"

"Declan." Wynona shook her head. "No. No one's gonna take you away from me. Pierce is a friend."

Declan pulled a chair out, but he didn't sit. Still focused on Pierce, he looked ready to bolt back up the steps.

"You're dating him?" he finally shot a look of disbelief at Wynona.

"We're friends," Wynona said calmly.

Pierce studied Declan closely as he finally lowered himself to sit at the table. Was he angry? Did the thought that Wynona might be dating Pierce upset him? True, Pierce didn't know the kid personally; he had seen him at the scene of the car accident, but he didn't know him to read him. So he couldn't be sure, but Declan didn't seem too bothered by the prospect.

"Pierce." Wynona looked at him with a tired smile. "This is my son, Declan Herzog."

"Hey." Pierce nodded at him and reached over the table to shake the kid's hand. Apparently surprised by the gesture, it took Declan a moment to respond. His grip was strong and dry as he shook hands, his smile small but more shy than cocky.

"Hi."

"I brought pepperoni and sausage."

"And green peppers," Wynona added pointedly. Pierce couldn't help but smile when Declan gave her an eye roll.

"And wings," Pierce added.

"Oh." Declan eyed the wings when Pierce took the cover piece off the foil container. "Those look good."

"Pierce is a firefighter," Wynona told him.

Declan nodded, but he was still thinking about the wings. Pierce figured if he'd had anything to do with the garage fire, he would look guilty. Or worried. But he didn't look like anything but a hungry teenaged boy ready to dig into wings and pizza.

"Cool." He glanced at Wynona. "Can I have a soda?"

"Yeah."

Pierce watched Wynona stand when Declan did. She pulled a drawer open, rummaged through the serving utensils and finally grabbed a pie server. With her free hand, she grabbed a stack of napkins from the drawer next to the utensils and put them on the table as she sat. Declan returned to the table with a soda. He popped the top on the can as he sat.

"So, do you like it?" Declan directed the question at him. Pierce hesitated and finally decided he was asking about firefighting.

"I do." He nodded. "I'm a volunteer, though. My day job is Lockland Distilling."

Declan arched his eyebrows as he reached for a wing.

"Why would you do that as a volunteer? I mean…it's a dangerous job, right?"

"Can be," Pierce agreed. "But it's important to me. I'm sure you've noticed Rodey is a tiny little spot on the map—"

Declan snorted. "No shit."

"There's a lot of little towns here. Lot of little townships. And a lot of distilleries. Know what that means?"

"Happy populations?"

Pierce laughed and looked at Wynona. "That was good."

Wynona shook her head.

"The possibility of fires is very high. All the rickhouses and barrels of whiskey out in the middle of nowhere. The community needs the township fire departments, and the township fire departments need volunteers."

"So, you do it for the community?" Declan sounded interested. "Or the bourbon?"

"Both." Pierce shrugged and tossed his hands palms up as if to say *what do you think?*

To his relief, Declan cut loose with a real laugh.

"What are you interested in studying?" he asked him after a few moments of quiet.

The kid stared at the wing for a moment and finally lifted it one-handed to his open mouth and sunk his teeth into it. He chewed and swallowed, a pensive look on his face.

"I don't know. I used to think engineering." He wiped his mouth with a napkin and then pursed his lips. "Now I'm not sure."

"Really?" Wynona served Pierce a slice of pizza and then put a piece on her plate.

"I don't know." Declan shrugged. "The ag and chemistry stuff here is interesting."

"I'm sorry," Wynona frowned at him. "What?"

"I mean, I like the idea of distilling."

"Since when?" she asked.

"I don't know. Some of the guys at school talk about it. Like their dads work at distilleries and stuff. It sounds kind of cool."

"It is," Pierce agreed. "But engineering is, too. Takes engineering to understand how to put up a rickhouse."

"Mmm." Declan raised his eyebrows. "That's true."

"Are you a junior?"

"Sophomore."

"So, you'll need to start looking at schools next year."

"I guess so."

Pierce and Wynona exchanged a look.

"You should come see me at Lockland someday. I could show you around the property."

"Really?"

"Yeah."

"I don't have to be twenty-one?"

Pierce flinched. "I'll see what I can do. You definitely wouldn't be tasting anything."

"Thanks, man."

twenty-two

. . .

WY

"Thank you."

Pierce tipped his head and studied her across the table. One small triangle of pizza—cheese and grease congealed now—remained in the box, pushed away to the side of the table. The wings were gone; Declan had wolfed down several. The cast hadn't hampered him. But Pierce didn't seem to mind. He had been a growing teenage boy once, and he probably could and would have done the same. Once Declan had focused on eating, Pierce and Wynona carried the conversation. Wynona had questions about the area, the history of Rodey, the bourbon trail itself, and how often Pierce went to Louisville or Lexington. Pierce asked her questions about her work life, thankfully leaving her personal life with Zach alone.

She knew there were things he would want to ask, but she appreciated that he hadn't in front of Declan. Pierce had also been interested whenever Declan did lift his eyes from his plate and contribute to the conversation. Dec had paid attention to Pierce's history lesson, and he had been interested in the bourbon trail and distilleries. But when he brought up the engineering and robotics camps he had attended when he was in middle school, Pierce had listened closely and tossed questions back at him. Wynona remembered a time when Declan was interested in building roller coasters and theme parks, even water parks. She had always reminded him that it was more likely he would be building parking garages and office complexes if he went into civil engineering. But tonight, she thought she had seen the wheels turning in Declan's head. She doubted he was interested in the bourbon itself; to her knowledge, he hadn't ventured into that sort of rebellion yet. He seemed genuinely curious about the design and construction of rickhouses and the distillery buildings themselves.

"Thank you," Pierce said quietly.

"For what? You bought and delivered dinner."

"You welcomed me into your home and let me meet your son."

Wynona smiled and relaxed back in her chair. Declan had stayed at the table for a bit when he decided he was full. And he had been polite, courteous. She was shocked, and she was tempted to be suspicious. But he had seemed genuine, so for now, she chose to believe he enjoyed meeting Pierce.

"Tonight wasn't the status quo," she promised with a small laugh.

"He's a teenager." Pierce shrugged. "What do you expect?"

"A little respect would be nice."

"True." Pierce nodded as if to grant her a point. "I got in trouble some when I was a kid, but respecting my mother was bred into me from the moment I took my first breath."

Wynona flinched. "Yeah. That's the problem. Zach certainly never modeled that behavior. And as I said, rather than insist it change or leave, I lowered myself to the same level."

"You did leave," Pierce reminded her.

"Not soon enough." She cleared her throat.

"How long have you been divorced?"

"Not long," she answered. "The ink might just be dry on the papers. But, Zach and I have been over for a long time."

"Do you still love him?"

"No." She sighed. "No, I don't. Haven't for quite a while. Things were ugly. For far too long."

"Do you plan to fall in love again?"

She wasn't sure if it was the question or the intensity in his gaze, but heat engulfed her just as surely as if Pierce had lit a match to her hair.

"You can't really plan for that, can you?" Her answer was no more than gruff whisper.

Pierce nodded as if to concede the point.

"Do you want to?"

Eyes locked with his, she took a moment to think. To burn. To want. No question she was attracted to the guy. Who wouldn't be? If Wynona gave herself permission to fantasize, she would definitely think about climbing Pierce. Wrapping her legs around his waist. Exploring that broad chest with her hands. Her mouth. Tasting the skin on his neck, feeling the flutter of his pulse on her tongue.

She was beginning to like him. As a person. If asked, she would probably consider Pierce Rooney a friend now.

But did she want to love him?

Because that was what he was asking, wasn't it? Sure, he had phrased it as a general question. But Wynona hadn't been out of the dating game long enough to forget how this stuff worked. Pierce was flirting with her. Maybe he wanted more than a quick fling. Maybe not.

The trouble was Wynona didn't know what she wanted. A quick fling? Well, she wouldn't run from the idea. It had been far too long since she'd had any fun, even longer since she had been touched with love. Since she had wanted to be intimate with anyone. But a quick fling in a town like Rodey, Kentucky, would most likely prove disastrous.

She would run into Pierce everywhere she went. She already did. And the women she had begun to think of as friends—every one of them—had some kind of tie to the guy. There would be no escaping him.

Not to mention Declan. She hadn't dated anyone since the divorce. There hadn't been time to think about it. But Wynona couldn't bring a man like Pierce into her home and introduce him to her son and then pretend it never happened once the sheets cooled. Maybe some women could do that, but Wynona was not one of them.

Love?

Sure, she hoped there would be love again. Someday.

But was thinking along those lines too soon? Too soon after the divorce? Too soon after meeting Pierce only a few weeks ago?

"I would love to know what's going on inside that head of yours." Pierce spoke quietly.

She ducked her head, but not before offering him a small smile.

"I don't know, Pierce." She shook her head.

"Well, you thought about it too long to tell me no." He shrugged when she peeked at him again. "So, I think that maybe somewhere inside you, there's a woman who wants to be loved again."

Her throat was dry when she tried to swallow.

"There might be," she admitted. "But I'm not sure I know her anymore."

Her heart hammered in her chest when he grinned.

"Well, then, Wy, maybe you and I can get to know her together."

twenty-three

. . .

PIERCE

He hooked the heel of his boot on the rung of the barstool and lifted the longneck bottle for a drink. The Bourbon Boot Scoot did a good business; even weeknights tended to bring a decent crowd. Sometimes the place was so packed on weekends, there was standing room only. The band took up the front corner of the place, but no one would complain about that. Pierce hadn't ever heard a band here he didn't like.

"So, are you dating her?" Mav asked.

Pierce swiped the back of his hand over his mouth as he swung his gaze back to his friend. Over Mav's shoulder, he saw the door open, and two of the Lockland brothers come inside. Branch, the eldest, gave him a nod when their eyes met across the room. Pierce gave him a quick wave and then focused on Mav again.

"No."

"No?"

"Not dating." Pierce shrugged. "But."

"But you've marked your territory."

"Don't be a dick." Pierce rolled his eyes. "I haven't touched her."

"I'm not being a dick." Mav shook his head. There was no bullshit promise or honor thing invoked, just Mav picking at the label on his bottle. Funny, the absence of the big macho bluffing made Pierce believe him. "Just curious. Everyone's settling down. Just figured you were next."

"None of the Locklands are settled."

"Matter of time." Mav shrugged. "Rye's talking about getting married. Taj and Rhett are both tied down."

"I think when a guy reaches that point in his life, he doesn't consider it being tied down," Pierce mumbled.

"See." Mav tipped his bottle at him. "You're thinking about her."

"I am," Pierce admitted. "But she's got a lot going on. She doesn't need me nagging her for a date."

The door opened again, and a loud whoop of conversation and laughter burst out over the band's current song. The Grassland Kings were doing an Alan Jackson cover; Pierce thought they sounded okay. But at the new noise, both he and Mav turned to see the girls crash into the Boot Scoot, all of them wearing big smiles with their boot cut jeans and heeled boots.

"Lot going on, huh?" Mav asked with a pointed look.

But Pierce was happy to see Wynona with Marlowe and the gang. All of them were dressed for a night out, hair and makeup just so. Wy's smile was as warm and genuine as the rest of their smiles. She needed these nights before she could commit to anything else. Maybe Mav wouldn't get that, but he did. Until Wynona settled here, until she was content with who she was and satisfied that Declan was thriving, she wouldn't give him the time of day.

He respected that.

Didn't mean he wasn't wishing time away, but he respected her love for her son and her sense of responsibility.

"Hey!" Summer called when she saw him and Mav at the bar. She led the group of women through a throng of people to join them. "Hey, Mav."

"Lockland hour," Mav announced with a nod down the bar to where her brothers Branch and Knox stood with pint glasses in hand.

"I'm a Bailey," she reminded him with a wink.

"Pierce." Marlowe nudged him as she sidled up to stand by him.

"Where've you ladies been?" Mav asked them.

"You look like you've been up to trouble," Pierce agreed, shooting a grin at Wynona.

"Well, my wonderful mother-in-law is babysitting. And since she has a ton of kids there between mine and Marlowe's, Declan is doing her a favor and hanging out there, too. Watching the kids."

Wynona locked eyes with him and arched her brows. No doubt Declan might be helping Claire Bailey, but also, Claire Bailey was babysitting him and keeping him out of trouble. Taj Bailey's family had always been a class act, but just now, Pierce felt a jolt of gratitude. Then again, why should he be surprised? People in this area tended to look out for each other. Of course, Claire Bailey would do what she could to make Wynona feel welcome and get her out of the house.

"Nice." Mav nodded.

"Where's Taj?"

Summer, elbows on the bar now, glanced at Pierce.

"He, Rhett, and Trey stayed at the Iron Stag," she answered.

"Probably hoping some other women will ride Bogart," Sheridan mumbled.

"Whadday'all want?" Summer looked over her shoulder at her friends.

"You guys were at the Stag?" Mav asked.

"Mmm." Marlowe nodded. "I would've complained, but Bristol rode Bogart. Haven't laughed that hard in ages."

Pierce snorted and looked from Marlowe to Bristol. Tried to imagine either of them on Bogart, the mechanical bull. Failed. Apparently, Rye's girlfriend Chantele had ridden Bogart the night they met. Never seemed to be any fun women looking for a good time in the Iron Stag when he was there.

Bristol laughed and shrugged helplessly. "Not cut out for bull riding. We'll leave that to Taj."

"Mmm. Mmmm. Mmmmmm." Summer quirked her eyebrows and plastered a dreamy smile on her face.

"Gross." Sheridan shook her head. "Gross. And gross. Stop sexualizing my brothers, you two!"

"Really?" Bristol shot Sheridan a look of disbelief. "Weren't you the one telling the story about Trey going down—"

Sheridan struck like a snake. Pierce and Mav laughed as she hooked her arm around Bristol's neck and clapped her hand over her mouth. Bristol snorted, laughing behind Sheridan's hand. Sheridan, face beet red, glanced at Summer.

"Put something in her mouth." She let go of Bristol. "Now."

"Not my job." Summer shook her head.

"And here we go." Sheridan laughed and rolled her eyes. "It never stops with these two."

"She's right," Marlowe agreed. "But it doesn't bother me."

"Yeah, well, they're not sleeping with your brothers."

"So, you left the guys at the Stag? Really?" Pierce asked.

"We came here to dance!" Summer lifted her fist in a big whoop motion. "Wynona has not danced in years. So, we wanted to make sure she still knew how to do it. Make sure she didn't have any old moves like the swim or something."

"Taj can dance," he said with a shrug.

"God, can he dance." Summer waggled her eyebrows.

Sheridan leaned past her sister-in-law and hollered at the bartender. "Please. I beg you. I need something to drink, and these two need something to keep them quiet."

Trent Ashburn met Sheridan's eyes and nodded. "Gotcha. Give me a minute."

twenty-four

• • •

WYNONA

The whole night had worked out like magic. When Bristol had called her earlier to invite her along for a girls' night, Wynona had tried to beg off. She couldn't possibly take off and leave Declan home alone for the night. God only knew what the kid would get up to while she was gone. But Bristol had the perfect solution. Since Rhett's mom was babysitting Taj and Summer's kids and Marlowe's son, she needed *help*. Wynona hadn't been sure Declan would go for it, but when she asked him, careful to phrase it that way, he had agreed.

Somewhat reluctantly, she thought. But she wasn't going to be choosy. A night out with friends sounded so good, she might have begged Declan to go to Claire and Waylon Bailey's house if he had argued. Apparently, he had decided a night with near strangers—he'd met Claire and Summer in Kissing Springs the week before—would be preferable to yet another night stuck at home with his mom.

The Iron Stag was nothing more than a country tavern with a cement floor, a rundown exterior, and yellowed light fixtures in the women's room. And cold beer. Wynona had loved it. It was interesting to see Marlowe's workplace and even more interesting to hear some of her tales about their regular drunks.

And the guy she had met and danced with last Christmas. Cass. When Summer and Sheridan pressed her, she had admitted that she and the guy had shared some kisses, but nothing more had happened. He was currently in Europe, but he and Marlowe kept in touch.

When Bristol decided she was going to ride Bogart, the rest of the girls—Wynona included—had cheered her on. Bogart had thrown her pretty quickly, but Bristol had gone down laughing. Sheridan tried to talk her into it, but Wynona had passed. Nothing like getting too crazy on her first real night out. Especially after the trouble Declan had gotten into. So, Sheridan talked Marlowe into it. The trouble with that being that she worked there. Probably had ample time to ride Bogart, to practice, if she chose.

At least that's what Wynona told herself. Marlowe had mounted the damned mechanical bull in her boot cut jeans and slinky black tank top and put on a show that had all the guys in the bar drooling. Summer and Bristol had pretended to tackle her when Bogart slowed and finally stopped, all of them laughing like schoolgirls.

Sheridan had suggested the Bourbon Boot Scoot for dancing. Taj and Rhett begged off. Taj had handed his keys over to Summer; the girls had piled into their SUV and driven to Kissing Springs.

She hadn't danced in ages. Wynona used to dance with Declan when he was little. When he was four or five, they would dance around the house together. When he was an infant, she would put on her favorite music and dance with him. But outside of that, it had been years. She and Zach hadn't danced since his sister's wedding, and she got married when Declan was seven.

Still, all the moves came back to her as she moved on the dance floor with her friends. Not that she was ever a good dancer. But the muscle memory and the rush of joy made her forget feeling self-conscious. She was out to have fun, to cut some tension, and get to know her friends better.

Never mind that Pierce Rooney was here. At the bar. They had talked for a minute. Pierce had greeted with her a warm smile, told her he was happy to see her out and about. He had asked after Declan, nodding his approval when she told him about Dec's reluctant choice to go to the Bailey's house, reiterating everyone else's opinion that the Baileys were good people.

But she felt his eyes on her as she danced and talked with her friends. Knowing he watched her made her body flush with that same heat of attraction that had swallowed her just last night, when Pierce had asked her if she wanted to love again.

She had dreamt about him. Nothing sexual, surprisingly. But she had dreamt about walking around the distillery campus with him, listening to him talk about the process of making bourbon.

Wynona wasn't any more ready to fall in love with anyone tonight than she had been last night. But she was feeling things she hadn't felt in a long time, and damned if that didn't feel good. Make her want more.

"I need a time out," she argued when the band started the next song. She had never heard of The Grassland Kings before tonight, but she loved their sound. After dancing to an Alabama cover followed by a Brooks and Dunn cover, she needed a breather. And a quick trip to the ladies' room.

"I gotta pee," Bristol announced.

"Me, too." She nodded and followed her off the dance floor.

The music wasn't as loud in the back corridor where the restrooms were. It was cooler there, too, after the press of bodies on the dance floor and the dancing itself. Both of them ducked into the ladies' room and claimed a stall. Bristol chattered about taking Wynona to see the male revue one of these nights. When they had first mentioned the all-male strip show, Wy had forgotten what Rhett told her and mistakenly thought Summer's husband Taj was part of it. She couldn't imagine ogling her friend's husband. The relief she felt when they told her Taj had never actually been part of the revue, that he had only done a few parties, was short-lived.

She'd done those things when she was younger. Strip clubs. Crazy parties. A couple of one nighters. But then she and Zach got engaged, and she got pregnant, and that was that. No more wild nights for her.

Wynona couldn't imagine being that person again. That woman that Pierce wanted to get to know. But tonight, she wanted to try it. Find herself. Be happy. She had more than enough love in her heart for Declan and a significant other.

As they made their way back to the bar, the lead singer of the band announced they were going to take a break. Pierce noticed the two of them and slid off his seat with a nod at her. Wynona smiled as she climbed up to sit where he had been.

"Ready for another drink?" He leaned close when he spoke to her, even though it was much quieter now that the band had stopped.

"I'm good for now," she shook her head, "but thank you."

Pierce tipped his head to her but the smirk on his face made her belly flutter with nerves.

"What?"

"If I can't buy you a drink, I'm gonna have to insist you dance with me."

"Dance with you," she repeated like she had to think about it.

"Mm-hmm. What's your favorite song?"

"What? You're gonna just think it and make it happen?"

"Nope. I'm gonna go bribe the lead singer to play it."

Wynona cleared her throat and licked her lips nervously. She wanted to dance with him. She would no matter what the band played next. But the thought of Pierce marching over to the band and asking them, bribing them, to play whatever she wanted was a bit of a thrill.

"I like John Michael Montgomery."

"All right." He nodded. "Don't move, Wynona Herzog."

She held her breath when he hesitated. The look on his face broadcasted his thoughts. He wanted to kiss her. What took her by surprise was that she wanted him to kiss her. When he simply tipped his head and walked away, Wynona swallowed down her disappointment. She wasn't one for public displays of affection. But now that she knew him better, now that he'd given her that look, she craved a soft, sweet kiss. Just the softest press of his lips to hers.

Her cheeks flushed as she watched him walk away from her. Dressed in dark wash jeans, a black t-shirt, and a red button-down shirt over it, he was easily the hottest guy in the place. The denim hugged his powerful looking thighs. His backside.

Realizing she was ogling Pierce Rooney's butt as he crossed the Boot Scoot, Wynona snapped herself out of her thoughts. And found her new friends watching her with big grins.

"He's pretty hot," Marlowe said with a nod.

"No." Wynona shook her head. "No. Not like that. We're just friends."

"Oh, no," Marlowe argued with a wink. "See, now, Pierce and I are just friends. Good friends. Know how I know it's more than that for him with you? He's never looked at me like that, and as hot as he is, I've never wanted to take a bite out of that—"

"Marlowe Jane." Summer shook her head.

"Shoulder," Marlowe finished indignantly. "I was going to say shoulder."

"You weren't." Sheridan, head turned in Pierce's direction, narrowed her eyes. "Not that I blame you."

"He's a good guy, Wy," Marlowe said quietly.

Wynona met her eyes and nodded. While she liked Marlowe and enjoyed hanging out with her, Wy wasn't sure if her friend was pushing her to look at Pierce as more than a friend or warning her that she would have hell to pay if she hurt him.

twenty-five

...

PIERCE

As it turned out, The Grassland Kings was now his favorite band. They had played not one but several John Michael Montgomery songs after he mentioned it to the lead singer. Once he coaxed Wynona out on the dance floor—she hadn't resisted, but she had been a bit shy—Pierce had slipped his arms around her, hoping to never have to let her go.

He even stayed on the floor with the girls when the band kicked it back up to some fast-paced song. Mav joined them. The Bailey brothers ended up showing up at the Boot Scoot and joining them. Taj had turned on some moves, though thank Christ he kept his clothes on. Still, the women had all whooped and hollered.

All except Sheridan who had laughed and buried her face in Trey's chest, eyes squeezed closed. As if that wasn't weird. Hell, Pierce loved the whole damned gang. They'd all been friends of some sort through the years. He understood how weird it was for Sheridan to see her friends get sexy with her brothers. He might put a fist through the wall if he saw some guy put the moves on Lyndi. And he might throat punch one of his friends if one of them happened to be that guy.

But seeing Sheridan and Bristol's ex so cozy, in love, blew his mind. The way Bristol talked, the guy had been a dick to her. He had waited for a while, after Trey and Sheridan started seeing each other. Figured they had done the drunk one and done, and the guy would end up fucking her over and walking out. But they had slipped down to the justice of the peace and tied the knot, much to Claire Bailey's chagrin. Trey was still around a year later. Still very much in love with Sheridan.

And Bristol and Rhett seemed okay with it.

One big happy family.

"Isn't that your sister?"

Speaking of which. Pierce looked down at Wy's fingers on his shoulder when she tapped him and then to the door as his sister walked into the Boot Scoot. Alone. He hated that. She had stuck out like a sore thumb when she was younger. No one actively disliked her. She just hadn't fit in with any particular group.

"It is." He nodded.

Sporting skinny jeans, heeled boots, and a black leather blazer over a crème-colored t-shirt, Lyndi held her head high as she made her way through the crowd to the bar.

"Wow."

"Wow, what?" Wynona asked.

Pierce spun them around a bit so he could watch his sister. She flashed Trent Ashburn a cool smile and said something to him. The guy nodded and set about fixing her a drink.

"I haven't seen Lyndi wear anything but combat boots since she turned thirteen."

Summer twisted to look over her shoulder and snorted.

"What?" he asked when she turned back to him.

"Little sister's all grown up in her fuck-me heels."

Pierce's laugh startled them both, but maybe not as much as what Wynona had said shocked him.

"I cannot believe you said that about my sister!"

Wy, clearly amused at his reaction, tipped her head back and held his gaze. "What? You think she doesn't do those things?"

"No." He frowned. "She probably just listens to My Chemical Romance and paints her nails black."

"And sleeps with guys she finds attractive," Wy added.

"Maybe," he conceded the point. "But that doesn't mean I want to think about it."

"Understood."

"She wasn't happy when she left Kissing Springs. I don't think she's happy now."

Wy's warm body pressed up against his was a comfort, bordering on a turn-on. If she moved just so, they would have a problem.

"It's hard," she said quietly.

"What?" He took a step back and stared at her with wide eyes.

Wynona eyed him suspiciously. "Worrying about someone you care about. Wondering if they're happy, and if they're not, how deep the unhappiness goes." She took a deep breath.

"Wanting to do anything you can to make them happy and not knowing what it would be."

Pierce blew out a sharp breath, nodded, and then choked on a small laugh.

"That's funny to you?"

"No. That's very true," he answered calmly. "Yes, I do worry about Lyndi. She's not even my kid, and I worry about her. So I get where you're coming from about Declan."

"But?"

He laughed again and tugged her the slightest bit to the right, sunk his hands into her hips, and pulled her close. Eyebrows quirked, he nodded when her mouth gaped open in surprise.

"Yeah. That." He swept his hand up her back and played with her hair. "That's what I thought you meant."

Wynona laughed and rested her forehead on his chest when she blushed.

"You know I want you."

"I do now."

He kissed her hair when he felt her laughter rumble up between them.

"You knew."

"I did."

"I'm sorry." He cleared his throat. "Natural—"

"Don't apologize," she said on a laugh. "I kind of forgot what that felt like."

Pierce drew away just enough to look her in the eyes when she lifted her head. “I’d be more than happy to remind you how all that goes. How it all feels.”

“I like the sound of that.”

“You wanna get out of here?”

Wynona’s laughter made her shoulders shake.

“What?”

“Isn’t that how Taj and Summer hooked up? Leaving here together for a one-night stand?”

“Maybe so.” He smoothed his hand around her neck and cupped her chin. “But look at where they are now.”

“Mmm.” Walking her fingers up his neck, she leaned into him and waited. Pierce brushed his lips over hers.

“I’m not asking you to go make out with me in my truck,” he promised. “Although, that idea is so good.”

“Then what are you asking, Pierce Rooney?”

“I don’t know. I just wanna go somewhere and be alone with you.”

Wynona quirked an eyebrow at him.

“We could talk.”

“You know if we walk out of here together, everyone in town will think we’re having sex.”

Pierce sighed and groaned.

“What?” she asked softly. “Change your mind?”

“Hell, no,” he barked. “But I don’t wanna walk you outta here and set the tongues a-waggin’. The old biddies in Kissing Springs run their mouths faster than damned cheetahs in a damned relay race.”

Wynona blinked at him. “Okay,” she whispered.

“What?”

“That’s quite a…metaphor?”

He laughed softly. “Whatever. I don’t want that to happen. Not with Declan. The last thing you need is for him to hear something unbecoming like that about you.”

“Okay, maybe you’re right,” she agreed. “But can you find somewhere private just long enough to give me a real kiss?”

twenty-six

• • •

WYNONA

Pierce led her back to the bar and asked the bartender for two beers. Wynona knew that he was playing it cool, moving slowly, nonchalantly so no one would notice them and decide they were up to something. It wouldn't matter to her if it weren't for Declan. But having rumors about her making out with some guy like a reckless teenager would do her son no good and make her look bad in his eyes. Not a good way to command respect from him. And she was ready to break out of that cycle.

Then again, her belly was buzzing right now with that anticipated kiss, and she felt all of sixteen, standing at the bar with him, elbow to elbow, counting the seconds until they could sneak off and be alone.

"Hey." Lyndi's face lit up when she saw Pierce. She picked up her cocktail and elbowed her way down to stand by them. Ordinarily, Wynona would be happy to see her, to talk to her. But at the moment, she was the epitome of a cockblock. Or something.

A misskiss maybe. Or a ziplip.

Knowing how ridiculous she sounded, even in her own head, Wynona took a drink of her beer and leaned into the bar as Lyndi and Pierce talked. If she wasn't careful, she might find herself leaning into Pierce. As much as she wanted to, she knew he was right. They had to be careful. The last thing she wanted to do was hurt or embarrass Declan.

"Are you meeting someone?" Pierce asked Lyndi.

"No. Why?"

"You're just here?" He frowned. "Like? What? Trying to pick someone up?"

"No. Just here for a drink, Pierce. You lived at home lately?"

Pierce's laugh was loud and genuine. "No. Point taken."

"Are you guys on a date?" Lyndi looked from Pierce to Wynona and back to Pierce.

"No. I was here with Mav. But then this lovely group of ladies came in, and this one rescued me."

"Mav's here?" She perked up and looked around.

"Don't even do that shit in front of me."

Wynona studied his face and decided he was serious. She had heard Mav Pressey's name often enough. She knew he was a tool. But it would surprise her to learn that Lyndi had been with him. There was a decent age gap between them.

"Relax, Pierce." Lyndi patted his chest. "It's all good. I'm having my drink and going home."

"Summer and Bristol are here."

Lyndi nodded. "I saw them. I'll talk to them. But I don't need a babysitter."

Wy held her breath for a moment. But when Pierce's sister looked at her again, Wynona simply returned her smile.

"Nice to see you, Wy."

"Okay." Pierce looked at Wynona. "You ready?"

"Where are we going?"

"To stroll the town square. Much quieter. But anyone who wants to know what we're doing just has to take a look."

Wynona hesitated.

"What? Does that worry you, too?"

"No." She shook her head. Really, she was curious about Pierce. His manners. His chivalry. His commitment to his community. How he was friends with someone who seemed to be the opposite. Wynona wasn't remotely interested in Mav Pressey, but it was fascinating to consider the differences between the two men.

"Wanna go out or not?"

She smiled. "I do."

Pierce took her hand and led her around the dancing crowd. She saw her friends gathered on the dance floor. Sheridan and Marlowe were having a ball together, Summer and Bristol both dancing with their guys now.

Wynona shivered when she followed Pierce outside. He let the door close and then shimmied out of his heavy coat. Before she could protest, he had balanced his beer in one hand while tugging the sleeves of the coat off and set it over her shoulders.

"Thank you." She smiled up at him.

"Wait." He stepped in front of her, cutting her off. Wy gasped, assuming he was going to kiss her. But instead, he put his bottle down and reached for the coat. "Put your arms in the sleeves."

She did as he asked and watched him zip it for her. The coat was toasty warm, but even better, it smelled like Pierce. When he reached down to grab his bottle again, she dipped her chin and breathed deeply of the spicy, soapy scent that was all Pierce Rooney.

"Think Declan's doing okay?" he asked her.

"If he wasn't, he would be texting me." She shrugged. "Every two minutes. In all caps."

Pierce shot her a look as they walked side by side across the street to the square.

"Haven't heard a peep."

"I'm guessing he's having a good time. Probably watching John Wayne movies with Waylon."

"He's supposed to be helping Mrs. Bailey."

"Claire," he corrected her. "And she doesn't need help. Kids love her. Now, he might, in fact, be following her around and thinking he's helping her just because he's smitten with her."

Wynona frowned at up him.

"Does that mean you had a crush on your friend's mom?"

He laughed softly. "Not exactly."

"You did, or you didn't?"

"When I was, like, eight? Maybe? But the Bailey boys would knock my teeth down my throat if I told you Claire Bailey is a very attractive woman."

“So, Dec’s gonna fall in love, huh?”

“You know.” He cleared his throat. “If you ever wanna get out…”

“Pierce.”

“With the girls. By yourself. On a date.” He shrugged. “And you would feel better if someone was kind of watching out for Declan, you can holler at me.”

“Who would I go on a date with?” She stopped walking. “If you were babysitting.”

“I wouldn’t be babysitting,” he argued. “I’d hang out with your fifteen-year-old son. We’d do manly things.”

Wynona sighed. “Declan would probably like that,” she admitted. “But I have no interest in dating anyone…”

Pierce arched his eyebrows.

“Else.”

The air was charged with electricity; Wynona could almost feel the vibration in her body. And yet, Pierce didn’t kiss her. Instead, he took her hand and started walking again.

“Have you been with anyone? Since Zach?”

Surprised by his question, Wynona didn’t answer immediately.

“I’m not asking for me,” he said simply. “But you. I don’t wanna move so fast, I scare you away.”

“I’m not scared, Pierce. Remember that? I handled Zach’s fists.”

Pierce studied her face for a moment. “I think you might be more afraid of this than you think.”

"What do you mean?" Her voice was gruff with emotion. She took a quick drink of her beer, and then stood frozen when Pierce took the bottle from her. He set both down on the sidewalk and turned to her. They were on the square, but they had walked through the middle to the other side. Still visible, if anyone was looking. Just a couple taking a walk. But not right out in front of the Boot Scoot, either.

Pierce cupped the back of her head in his hand and gently forced her to look up at him. Wynona had a moment to catalog his long eyelashes and thick, full lips before they descended and feasted on hers. The kiss was slow, torturously slow, but nothing about it was simple or casual. His tongue swept into her mouth in deep, powerful strokes. He curved his left arm around her shoulders, pulling her close, pressing her upper body to his. Even through his coat, and her blouse and bra, Wynona felt her nipples stiffen as his mouth claimed hers.

Conscious, suddenly, of her desire to kiss him, to own him, Wynona smoothed her hands up over his shoulders and linked her fingers at the back of his neck. She kissed him with the same emotion, the same depth, hungry to taste, to savor all of him.

When he broke the kiss, she tipped her head down, gasping to breathe.

"It's a small town, and I'm not interested in playing games," Pierce told her. "I won't push you, Wynona. But you know exactly what I want, and I know that scares you."

Wynona lifted her head and met his eyes.

"A little," she admitted. "I remember how it feels to fight. To take a punch."

Pierce pressed his thumb into her lip.

"But I don't remember this," she continued. "How it is to feel good."

twenty-seven

• • •

PIERCE

"So, you're dating her now?"

Pierce looked up from the cutting board where he currently held a lime to quarter. Knife in hand, he tipped his head at his sister and frowned.

"What?"

Lyndi rolled her eyes.

"Wy?"

"Mmm." He nodded. He was being deliberately difficult. It surprised him that tongues weren't wagging about the kiss he had laid on Wynona last weekend. At least, none until now. Someone was talking, though, if Lyndi was asking him about Wy. "No."

"Not dating."

"No." He returned his attention to the lime and slid the knife through it with ease.

"What bourbon drinks use lime wedges?" Lyndi scooted closer to him and watched him as he worked. "And what about kissing her the other night? In the square?"

"Bourbon Rickey." He kept his eyes trained on his hands. "Maple lime bourbon sour. Gimlet but switch the gin for bourbon. Bourbon marg—"

"I told you I slept with Mav," she reminded him.

"Unfortunately, you insinuated that you slept with my buddy, who is or was much too old for you, not to mention a player. And let's not forget that I didn't ask about you and Mav, so, why do you need to know about me and Wynona?"

"So, there is a you and Wynona." She beamed at him when he looked at her and rolled his eyes.

"We're not dating."

"Just kissing."

Pierce sliced each of the halves into half and stacked them at the side of the board.

"One kiss." He reached for another.

"Hell of a kiss from what I heard."

"Who'd you hear it from?"

"Does it matter?"

He shrugged. "No."

"Summer."

"What?" He sighed, frustrated, and turned to give her his full attention. "Did you guys whip out the binoculars when Wy and I left the bar the other night? We just wanted to talk. You kind of need quiet to do that."

"Mm-hmm." She nodded her agreement. "And kiss. You wanted to kiss her."

"I wanted to kiss her the first time I laid eyes on her."

"At the fire?"

"Second time I laid eyes on her," he corrected himself. If he remembered correctly, the first time he laid eyes on her—at the fire—he had wanted to shake her.

Don't forget, you accused her son of starting the fire.

Pierce narrowed his eyes and pushed the thought away. He had apologized for that. And he had met Declan, and he liked the kid. Sure, even Wynona admitted her son was a troublemaker, but now that Pierce knew them, knew him better, he understood the why behind the bad behavior.

"So, if you're kissing her, why aren't you dating her?"

"What are you? The dating police?" he snapped and turned back to the small pile of limes left to section.

"Nope. Kissing police."

Pierce snorted and rolled his eyes.

"I like her, Lyndi. But it's complicated."

"I like her, too." Lyndi sounded distracted. "I like being back. I wasn't sure it would go well."

"Yeah, well, if you're on the clock right now, it won't go well if a Lockland finds you in the bar harassing their star bartender."

"Not harassing Bristol," she answered simply. Pierce chuckled and looked up as Lyndi left the bar area. "But, yes, I should get back to work."

Pierce nodded and picked up another lime.

"Lyndi." His voice was gruff with emotion, something he wasn't entirely comfortable with. He and Lyndi had played when they were kids, though the age gap had been an issue even then. But in her awkward tween years, in his teen years, their college years—they had grown apart. He didn't know how to talk to her, and he doubted she would welcome his worry. He didn't know how to do it, but he would like to change things. "I'm glad you're back."

PIERCE SQUEEZED HIS EYES CLOSED BUT THE MENTAL IMAGE WAS still there. The candle, tipped on its side. The burned ruins of the woman's bedroom. Black ash covering the burned bed, the once white walls grimy with soot and water damage. Most fires he and his fellow volunteers faced were easy. A lot of them were warehouses, garages, other old buildings with antiquated electricity or kids messing around, and he had been part of the crew to battle the fire at the Brown Jug. But this one was bad.

Lola Shively hadn't made it out of her house. The elderly woman must have bumped the candle over to start the fire. As frail as she was, it would have taken her far too long to get out of the house, even if she went straight from her room to the door. Who knows if she had done that? If she had tried to put the flames out. From what they could tell, a Bible on the nightstand caught fire first, and the flames had jumped to the curtains. Hell, who knew? Maybe she had bumped the candle in her sleep, and it had taken a while for her to register that there was a fire? God only knew what she was doing with a lit candle. From what Pierce could remember, Mrs. Shively's memory wasn't what it used to be. No way should she have been burning candles at any time.

Maybe she had been confused. Waking up to a room filled with smoke and flames. Maybe she had tried to find her dog in the house or worried about kids. Mrs. Shively had lived alone out there on that gravel road for six years. Pierce knew her daughter had argued until she was blue in the face that she needed to move to a care facility. Obviously, that argument hadn't gone well.

Janet, Mrs. Shively's daughter, would probably lose herself in guilt now. That thought stuck in Pierce's crawl, just the same as the image of Mrs. Shively's motionless body on the floor in the living room. Those memories and the smoke had infiltrated his brain, his sinuses, his nose—the damned fire was three nights ago, and Pierce could still taste smoke.

He'd been in a mood since then. They all were. His brothers-in-arms might like the adrenaline rush of fighting powerful, roaring flames. But no one wanted injuries or death. Bristol had left him alone at work. Just laid her hand on his upper arm and gave him a gentle squeeze the morning after the fire. The Locklands had been equally respectful and supportive. Branch, the eldest of the brothers, had gone to school with Johnny Shively. He had died overseas. The family didn't deserve or need this added grief, that was certain.

Pierce hadn't seen Wynona since the night he had kissed her, but they had talked since then. They spoke on the phone the morning after the kiss. They texted often. But he hadn't talked to her since the fire. He wasn't up for it. Not just yet. Hard to pursue something fun, something that might deliver all the happiness he'd ever want, when someone else was grieving.

He wasn't a big drinker. Sure, he frequented the Iron Stag, but it was rare for him to be inebriated. He wasn't now, but he had downed more than his usual number of beers. Marlowe eyed him cautiously each time she filled his glass. She had forced him to eat a double cheeseburger and a plate of fries.

She had chattered his fucking ears off, talking about that night. The one when he kissed Wynona.

But Marlowe was relating events from the Bailey's house. Apparently, Way had been starstruck by Declan. Thought the older teenager was way cool. From what Marlowe said, Declan had been on good behavior. Way shared that they had ordered pizza, watched movies, and had popcorn. Taj and Summer's little girls had taken to Declan, too. Ellery had talked him and Way into coloring with her. Stella had tried to talk them into riding her stick horse, Rosie.

Pierce stared at Marlowe while she rattled. He appreciated what she was doing. The chatter might be making him crazy, but it was keeping his mind off Lola Shively. Mostly. It also made him feel good for Wynona. Maybe if Declan started feeling at home here in Rodey, she could relax a little.

Maybe if she could relax a little, the two of them could pursue what they started in the Kissing Springs Square.

"Hey."

Speak of the devil.

Okay, he hadn't been speaking, but Pierce turned his head to the left when he heard Wynona's voice. Hair clipped up in a messy twist, yoga pants, and an oversized sweatshirt sliding off her shoulder, she looked delectable. Pierce would much rather have had her than the double cheeseburger and fries.

"What're you doing here?" he asked with a frown.

"Mmm." She shrugged as she slid onto the barstool next to him. "I was in the neighborhood."

"Bullshit."

She laughed softly and eyed his beer. His glass was half-empty again.

"You okay?"

"Me?" He leaned back like he was dodging her question. "Fine. Why?"

Wynona tipped her head and turned that intense gaze on him.

"Why?" he repeated.

"You've had a rough week."

"Lola Shively had a rough week," he mumbled. "Fuck. Marlowe."

"What'd I do?" His friend appeared on the opposite side of the bar again.

"You called Wynona? Really?"

"You've had a lot," she said simply. "Better safe than sorry."

"You could've called Mav."

"And yet, I didn't." Marlowe shrugged and slipped away before he could say more.

"What's wrong with her calling me?"

"I don't need you here to take me home," he answered indignantly. "Yes, I've had a few more beers than I usually do. No, I'm not drunk. And where's Declan?"

"At home. Sleeping with his face in his history book."

"I'm fine."

"Let me just drive you home."

"Mm." He nodded. "And then what? You gonna come and get me and drive me to Lockland tomorrow?"

"If I need to."

Pierce closed his eyes and groaned.

"What if Declan wanders out of the house and steals a car while you're gone?"

"Wow."

He jerked his gaze to her at the hurt tone.

"I'm sorry. That was completely uncalled for. I just feel like a jerk that you thought you had to come and drive me home."

"We could talk," she suggested.

Pierce twisted his stool around and grinned. "Like, talk talk? Or talk like we did in the square that night?'

Wynona laughed softly.

"C'mon. Let's get you home."

twenty-eight

. . .

WYNONA

She sneaked a peek at Pierce as she put her car in reverse and backed out of her parking space. He might not be drunk, but he looked exhausted and somewhat tipsy. Not that tipsy was a good word for a man like Pierce Rooney. The second his denim-clad butt had hit the passenger seat, he put his head on the headrest and closed his eyes. Wynona gave him a quick once over, worrying about the firefighting thing. Had he ever been injured? Couldn't he die if the circumstances were…wrong?

She cared.

Beyond the whole humanity thing. Wynona cared about Pierce. True, they were only getting to know each other, but the more she knew of him, the more she liked him. And the physical attraction part was a no-brainer.

"Closed today, sweetheart," he mumbled.

Wynona snorted as she dragged her gaze up over his solid thighs and flat belly all the way to his slitted eyes.

"You wish." She looked at the windshield and steered out of the little gravel-pit-makeshift parking lot.

He laughed, but the laugh quickly rolled into a cough.

"Have you ever been injured?" she asked him, but she kept her eyes on the road.

"Mmm." He groaned. "Broke my arm in second grade. Fell off my bike. Sprained my ankles a lot in my football—"

"In a fire."

The quiet that answered lingered long enough that she peeked at him again. His face was averted toward the passenger window, but she could tell he was awake.

"Not really. Nothing serious."

"But you could be."

Pierce whipped his head around to frown at her. "Well, yeah. I mean. That's how fire works."

"Don't be a smartass."

"Sorry."

"I don't like it."

"Me being a smartass?"

"That you could get hurt."

"I'm tough, Wy. I'll be fine."

"Are you, though?"

She drove without asking for directions to his house. The little brick bungalow hunkered down between two other bungalows was dark. The whole neighborhood was quiet.

"How'd you know where I live?"

"Maybe I looked you up."

He smirked.

"She wasn't the first one."

Wynona pulled as far back in his driveway as she could and put the car in park in front of a neat, well-kept two car garage. Pierce looked around his small backyard when she killed the engine. The sounds of the car ticking thudded through her, loud and unnerving. She hated seeing Pierce like this.

"First what?"

"Body." He cleared his throat. "My first year…" He sighed and pressed his lips together. Wynona watched him struggle to stay in control of his emotions. His throat bobbed. He blinked a time or two, though she couldn't say his eyes were glassy. "There was a housefire that took a family."

Wynona winced when he glanced at her.

"Mom and Dad. Two kids. Eleven and five."

"That's awful," she said softly.

"Yeah." He nodded. "Yeah, it is. The one thing that got me through that was that they all went together. I can't even consider their fear…the way the smoke must have rolled over them and choked the life out of them. I can't consider the pain. The dad…" He shrugged and shook his head. "But you know. At least they died together. And if…there's an afterlife… they're together now."

Wynona reached over the console and touched his arm. "I like that. Makes something so horrible seem a bit hopeful."

"Mrs. Shively lived alone, and her daughter begged her to move to a care facility."

"Was she disabled?"

"No. She was old. Frail. And probably struggling with dementia."

"I'm sorry, Pierce."

"I can't help but think of how scared she must have been. How confused."

"Maybe you need to consider that she's in a better place now," she offered.

"Maybe." He nodded. "But I bet her daughter will blame herself."

"It's what we do," she whispered. "When someone we love is hurt."

Pierce pulled in a deep breath. Wynona watched his nostrils flare and then dropped her gaze to his chest as it expanded. She had wanted to touch him for days now. Hell, probably from the beginning. But that kiss had wrecked any control, any self-discipline she had.

But tonight, she wanted to comfort him, so she lifted her hand from his arm and stroked her fingers over the scruff on his face. Pierce leaned in as she did, and she kissed him. She pressed her lips to his, swept her tongue inside his mouth, and stroked him with her gentle need.

He shifted in the seat, but before he could touch her, she pulled away.

"What?" He shook his head, frowning when she reached for her door handle. "What about Declan?"

Wynona opened her door, climbed out gracefully, and hurried around to the passenger side of the car. Pierce remained frozen in the seat as she tugged his door open and slid in to straddle his lap.

"Jesus," he hissed.

"This okay?"

"This is more than okay," he answered. "But I do have a giant bed just inside the house."

"Shh." She laid her finger over his lips and then brushed hers across his cheek and down his neck. Pierce settled his hands on her hips. The only sounds in the car were their heavy breathing, the slide of her clothing against his coat. The small murmurs of appreciation from both of them.

"Wy." He lifted his hips when she unbuttoned his jeans.

"Let me."

"I don't have a condom on me."

"I'm on the pill," she promised as she unzipped his jeans and freed his thick cock from his briefs.

"You don't have—"

"Pierce." She shook her head as she pressed her knees to the seat and hooked her fingers in the waistband of her yoga pants.

"Is this a pity fuck?" he asked as she bared herself to him.

Locking eyes with him, she shifted and eased herself down over his erection. She was wet, but tight, and she felt every inch of him inside her.

"If you can't tell, I need this as much as you do."

"You're wet."

"I think I have been since you kissed me."

"What about—"

"Fuck me, Pierce." She licked her lips. "We'll worry about the rest tomorrow."

twenty-nine

. . .

PIERCE

The headache was minimal, and he remembered every bit of the night before. So, no, he hadn't been drunk. Yes, probably wise that Marlowe had called Wynona to give him a ride home, because drunk or not, he had been somewhat impaired. All the same in the eyes of the law. Pierce would've walked home before driving himself.

No hangover. Except for the memory kind.

Wynona Herzog had climbed into his lap and impaled herself on him last night. In her car. She had ridden him hard and fast, driving him out of his fucking mind with her tight little pussy, all wet and ready for him. Pierce shot his wad in record time. How the hell could he have held back? The woman had come onto him. She had taken control. She had kissed him. She had moved her body over him with finesse and purpose. Fuck, he'd only thought to cup her ass cheeks in his hands as she moved up and down over him. Her soft, warm skin and those firm cheeks had made him blind with want. But her heat, the way she worked his dick, had turned him to toast.

He hadn't seen her naked.

Hadn't touched her breasts.

Hadn't slipped his fingers inside her or over her clit.

He didn't even know if she had come.

It sort of felt like a pity fuck. But not really. He wasn't sure he'd ever had a woman that wet for him. Seemed unlikely for pity purposes. And yet, she had done it for him. That much was obvious.

Pierce loved it. Pierce had dreamt about the moment when he had exploded inside of her. He should probably change his sheets. He wanted more. And yet, he didn't know if she'd liked it. If she had come. If she would want to do it again.

For fuck's sake, he didn't know what the hell he was going to say to her today.

This morning.

Fuck.

He squeezed his eyes closed and lifted his hands to scrub them over his head. She was coming to pick him up so he could retrieve his truck. Dropping his hands, he looked at the alarm clock on his nightstand. Not quite seven. He had plenty of time.

"Jesus, man." He groaned when his dick jerked to life. Sure, he had time for that, but he didn't have the woman. He could take care of it himself, but he didn't want to. Not after last night. For one thing, after being inside her sweet little body, his hand wasn't going to do it. But mostly, not knowing if she'd had an orgasm made him feel guilty. He sure as fuck wasn't going to jack off to thoughts of her after as good as using her last night.

With that thought, he climbed out of bed and took a quick shower. Would she tell anyone? Not Declan. He knew she wouldn't have gone home and woke her son up to tell him she'd fucked Pierce Rooney in the passenger seat of her car. But what about Bristol? The rest of the girls?

He didn't care what they thought of his performance.

But he already had that dick move between himself and Wynona. All his friends had given him shit about accusing Dec of starting that fire. If they knew they'd had sex, and maybe Wynona hadn't enjoyed it, he'd have another strike against him. One more was a strike out, and Pierce wasn't ready to give up on Wynona. He wanted round two of their bodies connected. More intimacy. He wanted to kiss every inch of her skin and suck her nipples into his mouth and feel her pressed to him head to toe. In his bed. He wanted to wake up with her in his arms. To share pillow talk and breakfast in bed.

His phone buzzed on the counter. Pierce slapped the lid on his travel coffee mug and picked the phone up. Wynona had texted; she was waiting outside. Good thing he had skipped the wallowing and fantasizing and gone straight to the responsible adult mode.

He locked the door behind him and stepped outside. The air was a bit cool; he shivered in his flannel shirt as he made his way to the driveway. Or maybe that was nerves. He had no idea what to lead with.

"Hey." She offered him a smile when he yanked the door open to get in.

Hey? Good hey? Bad hey?

He smiled and returned the greeting. Exactly. Studied her when she backed out of the drive. She drove with her left hand; the fingers of her right were spread absently over her own travel mug. He smelled cinnamon, but he couldn't be sure if it was her coffee or her. The radio was on today; it hadn't been last night. Today, Wynona was listening to country music. Classic country, if he had to guess, because the voice singing sounded like Anne Murray.

"How's Declan?"

"Good. History quiz today," she answered. "I just dropped him off early."

"You took him to school early? Just so you could—"

"No." She rolled her eyes. "He asked me to take him early. He wanted to talk to his English teacher."

"Hmm." Pierce raised his eyebrows. "That's good. Right?"

"I think so." She shrugged.

They rode in silence for a moment, while Anne Murry sang about losing a dance partner.

"Wynona?"

"We did," she said simply.

"What?"

She looked at him, apparently amused by his confusion.

"We had sex in my car in your driveway last night."

He opened his mouth to answer her, but he wasn't sure what to say.

"I know," he finally mumbled. "I wasn't drunk."

"Are you upset about it?"

"I'm…" He frowned and shook his head. "I don't know what I am. But I think we should talk about it."

"Right now?"

"You wanna have lunch at the Skeleton Bar and talk about it then?"

"No."

Pierce sighed and sipped his coffee. The hot liquid burned his tongue.

"What does it mean?" he finally asked her.

"That we had sex?"

"I mean, I told you I wouldn't push you. And then the next time we see each other, you're on my cock like Taj Bailey trained you to ride bulls."

"Is that a compliment?" She shot him a frown.

"You bet the fuck it is," he answered.

"I'm on the pill."

"You said that," he reminded her.

"Look, I'm not afraid of men. Of sex. Not afraid of my ex-husband. I don't want him around, and I don't want him around my son. But I'm not *fragile*, Pierce."

"Meaning?"

"Only so many times a girl can touch herself and think about you before she needs more."

"Fuck." He groaned.

"Good fuck or bad fuck?"

"Best damned fuck ever," he answered, "and so were you last night."

She beamed at him, but Pierce didn't like how casual she seemed.

"I don't wanna fuck," he told her, his voice low and gravelly. "I want so much more from you."

"Me, too," she said softly. Pierce looked down when she moved her hand to link her fingers with his. "That's what last night was about."

"What do you mean?"

She glanced at him again, but this time, there was no self-satisfied smirk.

"You were hurting—"

"You said it wasn't—"

"And I wanted to remind you that sometimes life hurts," she continued, "but you keep going, and you find something that feels good. Here." She moved her left hand from the steering wheel and tapped her chest, over her heart.

"Wynona—"

She shook her head. "I'm not saying…I don't know if I'm in love with you, Pierce. Not yet anyway. But I'm kind of loving the idea of it."

He cleared his throat and squeezed her fingers.

"Well, I hope you plan to be with me again," he said quietly, "because I'm not sure you got a payoff last night."

The smirk was back.

"Are you asking if you made me come?"

"Nah." He shook his head. "I'm telling you I wanna take you to bed and make you come so hard, the walls come down."

The flush of pink in her cheeks made him laugh.

"What?" she asked as she looked out her window.

"The same woman who mounted me last night and rode me to the finish line is blushing about me making her come."

thirty

. . .

WYNONA

She didn't regret it. But she wasn't sure how she felt about it. No. No, that wasn't entirely true, either. That quick, intimate connection with Pierce last night had been incredible. Other than over in a heartbeat. She hadn't managed the pay off—Pierce's awkward worry over that still amused her. But she hadn't been worried about herself. She had wanted to pleasure Pierce. Not just to make him get his mind off the fire, the loss of life. But to remind him there was so much good in the world. That maybe there was something good coming for them.

Cue the unknown.

She had a little spring in her step today. No pay off last night didn't mean it was bad. Quite the contrary. Feeling Pierce inside her, nuzzling her nose, her lips to the warm skin of his neck, feeling the brush of his scruff on her face—all of it had been perfect.

But what she didn't know was *where they went from here.*

She wasn't in love with him yet. Being with Zach as long as she had taught her that much. She didn't know Pierce that well. Not half as well as she'd known her ex-husband and look how that turned out. But she wanted to learn him by heart. His hopes. His dreams. His regrets. His sorrows.

She wanted to know him and then fall in love with him. Pierce Rooney seemed like a good, strong man. Giving and compassionate, as well as willing to stand up for what he believed in.

Were they dating? No. After that scorcher first kiss, he had told her he wouldn't push her. As if he thought she was fragile. *On edge, maybe.* Worried that Zach would show up? *Maybe.* Worried Zach would hurt her? *No.* She didn't think he would lay a hand on her. Not now. But if he did, she'd go back at him in a heartbeat.

As long as Declan wasn't there to watch it.

Declan was her main concern. Zach would take him back to Sioux Falls with him over her dead body. At least if Dec stayed with her until he was eighteen, he wouldn't see more violence. More hatred. Maybe she wasn't enough for him. Maybe when he turned eighteen, he would vanish from her life. As much as she hated the thought, she thought maybe he could get out in the world and be happy. If he went back to live under the same roof as Zach, odds were he would end up being the same sort of man as his father.

The other thing, though. *That* weighed on her more than Zach right now. Declan's mental health. No right hook or sucker punch could hurt her the way Dec's words had the night he had said he would be better off dead. She still hadn't talked to Pierce about it.

And she wanted to. She wanted to sit with him and talk. About her fears. About her dreams for her son. Maybe even about some of those ugly memories with Zach. She wanted to know what Pierce feared. What he wanted in life. His favorite color and food. She wanted to lie beside him and whisper things of the heart.

She wanted to share with her new girlfriends, too. About what she had left behind. About her worry for her son. Not that she wanted to borrow a bullhorn and make her and Dec's business something for the old gossiping biddies to chew on. No. She was just ready to trust again. Ready to connect. To feel like she belonged to something. Someone.

Pierce didn't kiss her goodbye this morning when she dropped him off in the parking lot at the Iron Stag. In fact, he climbed out of her car without a word and swung the door closed. Wynona had waited, watched him start off toward his truck and then turn and come back to her car. He had sauntered up to the driver's side and waited for her to put her window down.

She had chills now thinking about him resting his forearm on the window frame, leaning down to look her in the eyes. His eyes had roamed over her face, her lips, but he finally met her eyes again. A George Strait song was playing; Wy wouldn't forget that.

"I'll call you." He tapped the top of her car as he stepped away. "Tonight. I'll call you tonight."

Wynona had nodded and silently watched him turn and go to his truck. When he was in the cab and the truck rumbled to life, she had pulled out of the lot, wondering if anyone had seen the exchange. Wondering if anyone assumed they had spent the night together. Wondering if she cared.

She did. And she didn't. Wynona had the feeling she and Pierce would be seeing a lot more of each other, so no, she didn't care what anyone thought of her being with him. But she didn't want her actions to come back on Declan. On the other hand, Pierce was well-respected in Rodey, in the surrounding area, so she hoped people would extend that courtesy to her as well.

Now, she was parked at the high school waiting on Declan. He probably wouldn't be happy to see her, but he hated riding the bus. She planned to drive on into Kissing Springs to pick up some groceries. They were down to one apple, the heel of the bread loaf, and they were completely out of milk. Wynona had worked all day, after driving Pierce to get his truck, though she had to force herself to concentrate more than once. She was ready to stretch her legs a bit. Maybe she and Declan could walk around the square once or twice before getting groceries. Again, she knew she wasn't his first choice of entertainment, but he might prefer that to going straight home and sitting around the house all evening.

When her phone buzzed with an incoming text, she took her eyes off the front of the school building to check it. She held her breath when she saw Bristol's name on the screen. Did she know already? Who would have told her? Wynona was certain Pierce wouldn't blab a word to anyone about what they'd done last night.

She tapped on the message only to find an invitation to the Bailey family Thanksgiving for her and Declan. Wynona laughed softly, though her eyes burned a bit with tears. Gratitude. It was nice to have friends again. Zach had kept her pretty isolated for most of their marriage. There was no way she could go back to the friends she'd had in high school, the friends she had had when she and Zach were first together. Either they had tired of her refusal to leave Zach and their disastrous marriage, or they had chosen Zach's side on everything.

She loved that Bristol had included her, and she figured Mrs. Bailey—Rhett's mom—had suggested it. The woman had been lovely when Wynona met her at French Kiss Coffee a few weeks back. Without even wondering what Zach would be doing for the holiday, she tapped out a quick response to Bristol.

Thank you so much, Bristol. I really appreciate the invitation.

As she put her phone down, Declan yanked her car door open and dropped into the passenger seat. He slung his backpack down to the floorboard in front of him, maneuvered his seatbelt around his waist with his left hand, and turned to stare at her with that wonderful sullen teen look every kid wore this day and age.

"Hi."

He grumbled in response.

"How was your quiz?"

"Fine."

"And your meeting with your English teacher?"

"Fine."

Wynona sighed and put the car in reverse. In addition to the trendy sullen look, Declan had adopted the *fine* response to most questions a few years back. She considered asking him if he got into any trouble but decided against it.

"There's a formal dance in December," he announced suddenly as she pulled out onto the country road. Traffic was thick and slow, so she had time to run his comment back in her head and look at him to make sure she had her kid in the car and not someone else's.

"Yeah?"

"Mmm." He nodded.

"And…" She took a deep breath and plunged ahead. "Do you want to go?"

"I dunno."

"Okay."

"Some of the guys are going just to hang out. Like. As friends."

"Mmm." She nodded. "That's a good idea."

When he didn't respond, she glanced at him to see him shrug.

"Is there someone you want to ask?"

"No," he snapped. "Not really."

"Dec?"

"I mean." He rested his head on the seat and closed his eyes. "I don't even know how to dance."

"I could teach you."

"No."

"Okay."

"Where are we going?"

"We need some groceries."

"Kissing Springs?" he asked.

"Yep."

"Can we eat at the diner?"

"Hope's Diner?"

"Is there another diner?"

She swatted his arm at his sarcastic reply.

Her phone buzzed again, but this time it was an incoming call. She glanced at it in the console and saw that it was Zach.

"It's your dad," she told Declan.

He shrugged.

"Answer it. He probably wants to check in with you."

thirty-one

. . .

PIERCE

"Do you get a lot of snow here?"

Pierce looked up at Wynona before glancing out the window and shaking his head.

"Not really."

"I hate snow," she grumbled.

"I love it."

He laughed when she rolled her eyes.

"Had enough of it to last me a lifetime in Sioux Falls," she explained. He watched her sweep her gaze around the main dining area at Casa Roja. The Mexican restaurant was new to Kissing Springs, so he had done the same—looked around at everything: the bright colors, the paintings on the walls, and the sombrero light fixtures—when they first came in. But Wynona was checking on Declan.

This wasn't a date. Simply because Pierce had asked if Declan would like to join them for dinner. The kid had agreed. He had even worn a smile while doing so. But he had seen a school friend when they first came in, so for the time being, he was sitting at the Gordon table, talking to Tyler and his parents.

The sky had been spitting snowflakes most of the afternoon, but there wasn't enough on the ground to track a rabbit. Pierce didn't mind snow, but he didn't necessarily want an abundance of it, either. For instance, he would probably hate living in the Dakotas. Kentucky got snow, but it was rare for them to get blizzard-like conditions.

Pierce thought it might be fun to get snowed in.

With Wynona.

Maybe during the holidays.

"Were you ever happy there?" he asked when she finally turned her attention back to him.

"In Sioux Falls?" She smiled, seemingly okay talking about it. Pierce was curious about her past, especially her marriage to Zach. Try as he might, he couldn't begin to imagine Wynona being violent. Even if it was simply to defend herself. Not that he would ever judge her. A woman had a right to take care of herself and her child. If it meant physical violence, she had the right to throw a punch or whatever the situation called for.

She just shouldn't have to.

"Yeah." He took a drink of his soda and watched her expectantly.

"I was." She nodded. "I had good friends there. In the beginning. Zach and I had fun in the early years. But it got toxic. And a lot of my friends got tired of me, of my excuses for Zach's behavior. Of my promises to leave when I had no intention of walking away. And when things got really bad, a lot of my friends…well, they were married to Zach's friends."

Pierce pursed his lips and nodded.

"I was scared to leave," she whispered. "I mean, I loved him. Ya know? I loved him, and we were supposed to be a team."

Pierce wished he had magic words to say, but he could only reach over the table and touch her hand.

"And then, finally, I knew…things were bad. Ugly. So many times, I thought about leaving. About taking Dec and getting away from him. But it was like he would figure it out, and then he would turn on the charm. Not to mention, I was a single mom with nowhere to go. I think that love grew into resignation. So I started fighting back."

"I'm glad you did."

"I am, too, except that I probably messed my son up for the rest of his life."

"I don't think so, Wy."

She huffed out a long sigh and sat back on her side of the booth.

"I don't know what gave me the courage to finally do it."

"Declan."

"Yeah." She licked her lips. "Yeah. You're right. I just wish I had done it sooner."

"Stop beating yourself up over it," he said quietly. "You did what needed to be done. And now you're here."

"And my son is—"

"He's fine," Pierce interrupted her. "He's adjusting."

“I think I’m going to call the school counselor and see who he would recommend. You know. In case I could talk Dec into trying therapy.”

“Probably a good idea.”

“He’s just such a mix of wide-eyed little boy and hurt, angry teenager. I never know for sure which Declan I’m gonna get each time I see him.”

“This.” Pierce nodded his head toward the Gordon table. “Is a good thing. The Gordons are a good family. And Ty’s a good kid. He’s a serious baseball player. Smart kid. Does well in school.”

Wynona sighed again, this time looking relieved.

“My sister had a hard time here in Rodey. She was this tiny little—well, you’ve seen her. She’s like a pixie. And she had this huge attitude. Big personality. I wouldn’t say she was bullied here, but she didn’t fit in. She didn’t have people.”

“Other than you and your parents.”

Pierce shrugged. “She was close with Mom and Dad, but I wouldn’t say I did much for her.”

“I’m sure that’s not true.”

“I wish I knew her better,” he mumbled. “She lived, like, a whole life away from here. So much so that she’s ready to come back and settle in and live here again. Like she exorcised her demons or something. I wanna understand that.”

“Ask her.”

Pierce snorted. “She would probably deck me.”

“Pixie decks the jolly blonde giant.” Wy grinned.

“I’m not jolly.”

"Not the point."

"She slept with Mav."

"I'm sorry?" Wynona blinked at him. She sat forward again and selected a chip from the basket.

"Mav Pressey."

"The one you warned me about." Wy nodded. "Lyndi slept with him?"

"When she was younger. Like, before she left."

"Ooh. Ouch." Wy flinched. "Did you know?"

"Nope." Pierce drummed his fingers on the table. "If I would have, I would have kicked his ass."

"Understood."

"I just…I don't know. I've been watching Lyndi with my friends…and you know how they are. So, now, they're her friends. Which is good. I guess…I just see a woman who looks like my little sister, but I don't even know her."

Wynona looked up as Declan wandered back to their table.

"So, get to know her, Pierce." She shrugged.

Declan slid into Pierce's side of the booth. Surprised, but completely okay with it, Pierce simply scooted in to make room.

"You ready to order, Mr. Social Butterfly?" he asked the kid.

Dec grinned. "Yeah. I want the chicken taco dinner."

"How do you know? You haven't looked at a menu." Wynona crunched a chip and then covered her mouth with her fingers.

"It's what Tyler had. Looked good."

"Awesome." Pierce nodded.

"Tyler's one of the guys going to the formal," Declan told Wynona.

"Oh. Okay."

"Are you taking a date?" Pierce glanced at him.

Declan shrugged as if to dismiss the question. "Are you dating my mom?"

It was on the tip of his tongue to say no. He wouldn't push Wy, even after the little acrobatic stunt she had pulled in the front seat of her car the other night. But before he could open his mouth, Wynona nodded.

"Yeah. Pierce and I are dating."

thirty-two

• • •

PIERCE

"Not dating, huh?"

"Shut up." Pierce didn't spare Mav a glance. Word traveled fast. Mav was the seventh person today to ask him about Wynona. Not that he minded, but sometimes it was fascinating to try and track the gossip train. He doubted Wy had told anyone, simply because she worked from home. No one she worked with would spread the news here in Rodey. That left Declan. He had probably told a friend who told a friend who told a parent and on down the line. At some point Minnie and the rest of the old ladies in Kissing Springs would get wind of it, and he and Wy would be as good as married.

The thought didn't make him sweat bullets like it might have just a year or two ago.

"Guess that means you're off the market."

Pierce cut Mav an irritated look. They were friends, had been for a long time, but Pierce didn't paint the town with the guy often. It wasn't like they were drinking buddies who went out carousing every weekend.

"What?" Mav shrugged. "I'm heading to Nashville for a little vacation."

"Mmm." Pierce leaned his elbows on the bar and narrowed his eyes at Mav. "When did you mess with my little sister?"

Pierce wouldn't have thought it possible, but Mav actually flinched. His face paled as he stared back at him.

"She told you?"

"She did."

"When? Like, was she upset about it?"

"Nah." Pierce shook his head. "Not at all. Sounded like you were just a notch in her belt."

Mav snorted.

"How's that feel?"

"Look, I didn't want—she asked…It wasn't—"

"I don't want details, Mav." Pierce took a swig of his beer. "Or excuses. Or apologies. Or anything."

"Then why bring it up?"

"I dunno. Leverage, maybe?"

"I didn't hurt her."

"Again." Pierce squeezed his eyes closed. "Don't."

"Rye and Chantele set a date."

Thrilled at the change of subject, Pierce turned to look at Mav with a grin.

"Now, that's good news!"

"Next summer."

"Good." Pierce nodded. "I know he's crazy about her."

"Rye said Chantele's gonna have a big bachelorette party in Kissing Springs."

"Mmm." Pierce laughed. "Which means Nova Brathwaite will be back in Kissing Springs a few times in the next year."

Mav quirked his brows in response. The night Chantele and Rye met, she had her friends with her at the Iron Stag. One of them was married. The other was single, and she and Mav had enjoyed each other's company a few times since then.

"You ever think about settling down?" Pierce asked him as Marlowe approached on the opposite side of the bar.

"Nope." Mav shook his head. Marlowe only laughed at them.

"You're talking about Rye and Chantele."

"We are." Mav nodded.

"Pretty exciting." Marlowe grinned. "Soon enough you'll all be married. And I'm still gonna be standing here, tending bar."

"I will not be married," Mav corrected her. "Let's make a deal. If we hit forty, and we're still unattached, we do a beach vacation together."

"Not in your wildest dreams," Marlowe answered, though the smile on her face softened the blow.

"You hear Pierce and Wynona are a thing now?"

"Heard they're dating." She looked at Pierce. "Interesting."

"Why is that interesting?" Pierce asked with a frown.

"Well, it happened not long after she drove you home the night you were drunk."

Pierce snorted and rolled his eyes.

"I wasn't drunk."

"You were impaired enough you shouldn't have been driving."

He shrugged but kept his mouth shut. It was one thing for Rodey, for the people of Kissing Springs to know he and Wy were dating. But that didn't mean he had plans to share what had happened the night she drove him home.

"Patrick Hoffman and Declan Herzog got Dan Sorenson's horses all spooked the other night," Mav announced.

Pierce struggled to stay calm. This time, he knew the rumor was wrong. He and Declan had been working on his geometry homework at the time the kids were seen around the Sorenson's farm. Hell, the thing was, kids would be kids. Yes, Pierce would draw the line on some things—the car accident Patrick had caused when Declan was with him, for instance. Anything that would cause danger to someone else was off-limits. But yes, kids were going to make stupid decisions and do stupid things. And hurt themselves in the process.

And yet, Pierce was irritated that just because Patrick Hoffman and some of his buddies were out causing trouble on a random weeknight, everyone was going to point the finger at Declan just because he had already been in trouble. It irked him that everyone jumped the gun on the accusations. Reminded him, too, that he had done the same. Now he knew how frustrating it was for Declan and Wynona.

"Actually, Dec and I were working on his geometry homework," he said calmly. "When the kids were seen around the Sorenson's. So, while Dec has been known to break the rules and get in trouble, he didn't do it this time."

"Yeah?" Marlowe arched her brows. "You're helping with homework?"

"Math blows Wy's mind. I don't mind helping out."

"That's cool." She nodded.

"Gonna show Dec around the distillery campus this coming weekend. He's interested in engineering."

"Does he know where he wants to go for college?"

"No." Pierce finished his beer. "I'm not sure he's done a lot of looking. If you ask, his response is usually some variant of anywhere but here."

"Way wants to go to University of Kentucky. My dad's got him interested in agricultural economics."

"Good thing to be interested in around here," Mav agreed. "But it's kind of weird hearing you talk about Wynona's kid like that."

"Like what?" Pierce frowned.

"I don't know. Kind of parental, I guess. Like you're his dad."

Pierce sighed and shrugged. He would never try to step in and be Declan's dad. But because of the things he knew about Dec's father, Pierce had no qualms about being around for the kid if he needed something.

"Like Marlowe said, Mav." Pierce elbowed Mav as he stepped away from the bar. "The rest of us are growing up."

"Y'all have fun being responsible adults," Mav said with a grin. "I think I'll pass."

thirty-three

. . .

WYNONA

The Black Olive's lunch specials drew quite the crowd in Kissing Springs. Wy sat at a table with her new friends—there were six at their table—and every other table but one was occupied. The smell of garlic hung in the place; Wy's stomach had been growling since they had been seated. She had ordered lasagna at Sheridan's urging, but she knew others had ordered spaghetti, pizza, ravioli—she would have restaurant envy, that was certain.

"Where's Declan today?" Marlowe asked her from across the table.

Wynona glanced at Summer who sat next to Marlowe. "Pierce is showing him around Lockland."

"Really?" Sheridan sounded curious. "Is he interested in distilling?"

"Or just bonding with his mom's boyfriend?" Bristol added with a smirk.

Wynona chuckled. While Bristol was joking, Wynona hoped that Declan and Pierce had a good day. She would never act as if Zach didn't exist, she would never totally cut him out of Dec's life, but she loved the idea of Declan having positive male role models here in Kentucky.

"He's actually interested in engineering," she answered.

"Mmm." Summer nodded. "We'll get him roped in and transfixed by the whole business, and he can build us new rickhouses when he's out of school."

"Yeah." Wynona picked up her water glass for a sip. "I do think that intrigues him."

"Pierce is probably having the time of his life." Marlowe looked around the Italian restaurant before settling her attention back on their table. "He loves the distillery. I think he likes hanging out with Declan."

"They were meeting Branch there," Summer told them. "Branch was gonna talk about the whole distilling process."

"Good." Bristol nodded. "It's nice that Pierce and Dec get along."

Wynona looked up as their waitress approached the table with some of their orders. She had shared some of her stories with the girls, the bad things and memories from Sioux Falls. They knew she had learned to throw a nasty punch, and none of them seemed to judge her for it. Not that it made Wynona feel any better.

"It is," she agreed. "Declan needs to see the way other adults handle adversity. He needs to learn to channel his anger."

"Do you think that's why he gets into trouble?" Marlowe asked her. "Do you think he's angry?"

"I don't know how he couldn't be angry," Wynona said quietly. "I mean, I know kids do stupid things sometimes, and there isn't any deep-rooted psychological trauma that causes it. There's no life where Declan would be perfectly behaved. But, yeah, I think he's angry. At me. At his father. Because we hated each other too often. Too loudly. I think he's angry at me for not leaving sooner. And angry at me for leaving when I did. Taking him so far away from Zach."

"Does he talk to Zach much?"

Wynona glanced at Sheridan with a nod. "He does. They talk on the phone a few times a week. Zach has started talking about having Dec come for a visit around Christmas."

"Will you let him?" Marlowe asked her.

"I don't know." Wynona cleared her throat. The waitress had put down the plates she was carrying and gone back for more. Wynona watched her set her lasagna in front of her. She waited until they were alone before speaking again. "Declan started therapy. I'm not sure if it would be good for him right now or not. To see Zach. I guess I'll see what his therapist says."

"Who's he seeing?"

Wynona watched Bristol shake garlic salt over her personal pizza.

"Andrew Hartley. He's in Lexington, so right now, Dec goes every two weeks."

"Do you think it's going well?" Sheridan asked her.

Wynona stuck her fork in her lasagna but sat for a moment before answering. She didn't mind sharing this. In fact, she was relieved to talk to friends about her worries. She hadn't mentioned Declan's comment about having no reason to live, but just sharing that she was concerned about him and his mental health had helped. However, she didn't want to be the topic of every conversation with her friends, either.

"He's only been once so far," she admitted. "But he did seem to like the guy well enough. The counselor at Kissing Springs High recommended him."

"Good." Summer nodded.

"Did you guys hear that Chantele and Rye set a date?" Marlowe asked the table at large. Wynona met her eyes and gave her a tiny nod of thanks for changing the subject.

"No!" Bristol picked up a slice of her pizza and took a big bite. "That's exciting!"

"When're you and Rhett gonna tie the knot?" Summer asked her.

"I don't know," Bristol said around a mouthful. "Hopefully someday soon."

"What's their date?" Sheridan asked Marlowe.

"I think it's the third Saturday in July."

"That'll be pretty."

"And hot," Bristol mumbled.

"Have you met Chantele?" Marlowe directed the question at Wynona.

"No."

"She's a transplant, too. She moved here from Lexington after meeting Rye."

"We should invite her for the next girls' night," Sheridan suggested. "I know she goes back to Lexington a lot on the weekends to see her friends, but maybe she'd go out with us if we asked."

"We can do that," Summer agreed.

"Did you give anymore thought to Thanksgiving?" Bristol asked Wynona.

"Yes. I appreciate your invitation. But." She grinned. "Pierce invited me and Dec to join his family."

"That makes sense." Bristol nodded. "Anybody have to work on Black Friday?"

There was a chorus of nos around the table.

"Let's go shopping."

Summer agreed immediately.

"Sheridan?" Bristol tipped her head. "We could go to Lexington. Do some shopping. Come back here and meet the guys for dinner somewhere."

"Sounds good."

"Marlowe?"

"You know I hate shopping," Marlowe said with a groan.

"But you love us," Bristol beamed at her and continued, "and even if you hate it, you still need to find something for Way."

"Fine." Marlowe rolled her eyes.

"Lyndi?" Summer leaned around Marlowe to look at Pierce's sister. She beamed and nodded, though she had been quiet most of the day.

"Wy?"

"Sure." She nodded. "As long as I have some place for Dec to go."

"Well, if Pierce doesn't keep him busy, I'm sure my mother-in-law would like the help babysitting again."

Wynona glanced at Summer and nodded.

"I'll find out."

"Dinner at 214," Sheridan suggested. "We can make reservations."

"Perfect!" Bristol nodded. "And then drinks and dancing at the Boot Scoot."

"I love it when a plan comes together." Summer attacked her ravioli like she was starving. Wynona settled into the comfortable silence among them as they all turned their attention to their lunches.

She froze when she felt her phone vibrate in her purse.

"What's wrong?" Sheridan asked.

"Someone's calling." She put her fork down and reached for her purse hanging on the back of her chair. Bristol and Summer talked about something that happened at the Bailey's house the day before, and Sheridan and Marlowe were laughing together about something.

Dread knotted itself around the one bite of lasagna Wy had managed so far when she saw Pierce's number on the screen of her phone.

"Hey."

"Hi." He sounded happy.

"Hi. What's up? Is everything—"

"Everything's fine, Wy," he promised. "I just called to see how you're doing."

Her shoulders eased as the sudden tension melted away. She sighed in relief, and something else, something light and happy inside her made her smile.

“Good. We’re at The Black Olive.”

“Sounds good.”

“Making Black Friday plans.”

“If it involves shopping, count me out.”

Wynona laughed.

“In fact, me and Declan will find something to do while you girls are shopping.”

Wynona happened to meet Bristol’s gaze as she grinned at Pierce’s words.

“That sounds nice.”

“We’re good here,” he said again. “You enjoy your day with the girls.”

thirty-four

• • •

PIERCE

"Okay." Branch grinned at Declan. "I told you there would be a quiz on this. You ready?"

Pierce watched Declan duck his head, but he was smiling. "Guess so," he mumbled with a shrug.

"What are the requirements for making bourbon?"

Declan glanced at Pierce, but he only shrugged. Pierce was sure Declan would be able to answer anything Branch asked him. He had been very attentive to the whole tour of the place—from walking around outside the amphitheater, checking out the rickhouses, and the entire distillation process.

"Um. To be considered bourbon, it has to be made in the United States."

Branch, leaning on the bar in the tasting room itself, nodded.

"The mash bill has to be at least fifty-one percent corn."

"Yes."

"Distilled to a maximum of…a hundred and…sixty proof?" When Branch nodded again, Declan continued, "Barreled at a maximum of one hundred and twenty-five proof."

"Good."

"Aged in new oak barrels. And…"

"Yes, but technically, it doesn't have to be barrels. Any shape, but new American oak is important."

Declan laughed softly. "Can you see an American oak triangle?"

Branch grinned. "Anything else?"

"Ummm…nothing can be added. No flavoring or coloring."

"Right." Branch reached for a bottle of the flagship bourbon. "So, this is the part of a tour where we taste the whiskey."

Pierce coughed to hide his small chuckle at the look of surprise on Declan's face.

"I'm only fifteen."

"I know." Branch nodded. "But here's the thing, Declan. Growing up in my family, in the bourbon industry, my brothers and I, even my sister, tasted whiskey a long time before we were twenty-one. We weren't allowed to get drunk on it, mind you. But we started tasting young."

"Does my mom drink bourbon?" Declan directed the question to Pierce.

"I've seen her drink bourbon once or twice," he answered honestly. "But I don't think she's a fan."

Branch laughed. "Can't rope everybody into it, I guess. Then again, if you guys are seeing each other, maybe you can change her mind. So." Branch straightened from the bar. "You wanna small taste?"

Declan looked to Pierce, probably for an okay. Pierce wasn't sure what Wynona would say, but she had trusted him with her son for the day. She knew exactly where they were and what they were doing, and she hadn't said she didn't want him to taste anything.

Besides, Pierce believed tasting a high proof bourbon at a tender age like fifteen might keep a kid from hitting alcohol on a regular basis when he was underage.

"Taste it," Pierce told him.

The grin on Declan's face told him he had made the right decision. He just hoped Wynona wouldn't be angry.

Branch poured a half ounce into three different Glen cairns and explained to Declan as he did the purpose of the glass and how to nose the whiskey. Declan nodded along and swallowed hard when Branch and Pierce picked up their glasses.

"Let's send your mom a picture," Pierce suggested.

Declan kind of shrugged and picked his glass up. The three of them stood together, glasses in hand, and Pierce snapped a selfie. He sent it to Wynona with the comment that they were each having a very small taste of the flagship.

"Okay, so, look at the color first." Branch held his glass out and turned it this way and that. "What word comes to mind?"

"It's…not like super light, but it's not that really dark color like some whiskey I've seen."

"Right. Depends on how long it's aged in a barrel."

"Now you nose it," Pierce told Declan. "Yep. Smell it with both nostrils. Yeah. One at a time. Keep your mouth open."

Declan did as Pierce explained and drew away almost immediately.

"What do you smell?"

"Nail polish remover."

Branch chuckled. "Fair enough."

"I smell wood," Pierce told the kid. "And wood sugars."

Declan sniffed the glass again and shrugged.

"It's okay," Branch said simply. "You acquire the taste and the nose as you learn more about the process and drinking it. And while I did pour you a taste, we're not here to figure it all out today."

"Maybe in six years," Pierce added.

Declan only grinned.

"Okay, so you're gonna try to make that pour three sips. First sip is the acclimation sip. It's gonna burn. Your body's gonna say what the hell are you doing to me?"

"Great." Declan's mumble lacked any sting. He was still grinning from ear to ear.

"Ready?" Branch and Pierce lifted their glasses in unison. "Take a sip. Hold it for a few seconds. And then swallow."

When Branch and Pierce took their sip and put their glasses down, Declan took a deep breath and tried a sip. Pierce couldn't hide his amusement at the look of horror on Dec's face.

"Oh my God." He swiped the back of his hand over his mouth.

"You okay?" Branch asked him.

"Mmm." He nodded.

"Okay, now the next sip isn't gonna feel as hot. And you might be able to discern flavors."

Pierce's phone buzzed as Branch talked to Declan. He took a step away from the bar as he pulled the phone from his pocket and checked the screen. Wynona. He held his breath for a second, hoping she wasn't pissed about the whiskey.

"Hey."

"Hey. How'd he do?" she asked with a small laugh.

"I don't think he loves it," Pierce answered. "Dec, it's your mom. She wants to know what you think of the Lockland Five Year."

Declan took his second sip and tried hard to hold it and not make a face. Kind of made Pierce think of a little kid taking cough medicine and wanting to spit it out.

"Don't corrupt my kid. No more than he already is," Wynona warned him. Her tone was light; Pierce could hear the other girls talking in the background.

"He's fine."

"Did he enjoy the tour?"

"Yes. I think so." Pierce would expound on his answer later, when he and Wynona were together, and Declan wasn't within listening distance.

"Good. I think I'm going to head home soon. Sheridan had to cut out after lunch, and Summer's getting ready to head home, too."

"Okay. Dec and I will meet you at your house. Does that work?"

"Sounds good."

He pocketed his phone again and meandered over to the bar.

"Is she mad?" Declan asked him.

"No."

"Now, if she finds you hitting a bottle somewhere else, she's probably gonna be pretty pissed," Branch offered with a quick shrug. "Moms don't like when their kids drink. Bourbon moms deal with it for business reasons. But you're not gonna get by with it. Remember that."

Declan grinned. "I know."

"You have questions about anything?"

"Not right now," Declan answered. "But thank you. This is really cool."

"You're welcome. Make sure to thank Pierce, too," Branch said pointedly. "He took the time out to be here today, too."

"Dec and I had to find something to do today. The girls are all hanging out in Kissing Springs."

Really, it was the other way around. Wynona had to find something to do because Pierce wanted to take Dec out to the distillery. But Declan didn't need to know that.

"It was cool," Declan repeated with a nod.

"Most sophomores in high school don't get this opportunity," Branch told him.

"Yeah, I get it." Declan set his glass down on the bar, the last of the bourbon still a golden ring in the bottom.

"Hit me up if you wanna come out again and see stuff."

"Thanks, man."

"I'm gonna work a bit while I'm here," Branch told Pierce. "I'll see you tomorrow."

"I'll be here with bells on."

"Leave the bells at home," Branch argued. "See ya, Declan. Good to meet you."

"Thank you, Mr. Lockland." Declan reached to shake Branch's hand.

"Branch. Mr. Lockland is my dad."

They shook, and then Pierce led Declan out the side door, where tours entered the tasting room. Branch locked up behind them and waved as Pierce and Declan started walking.

"Anything you want to look at again before we leave?"

"Nah."

"What was your favorite part?" Pierce asked as they neared his truck.

Declan looked around the campus before settling his eyes on Pierce. "I dunno. I liked it all. I liked seeing how the whole process is chemistry."

"How do you feel about chemistry?"

"I got an A in chem. Can't say I was excited about it."

"Before now?" Pierce shot him a grin as they settled into the truck cab.

Declan secured his seatbelt with a grin. "The mold on the old rickhouses is cool. I see it all the time, but never knew what it was."

"It is cool. Some of the distilleries in the area have really old rickhouses. The big old buildings with all that mold on them look like something out of a horror movie."

"They do," Declan agreed.

"Do you remember what causes it?"

"Evaporation in the aging process. Right?"

"Yep. Remember what they call it?"

"The Angel's Share."

"I'd have to give you an A for the day."

"Is Mom home?"

"She was about to head home. So, I told her we would meet her at the house."

"Are you staying? Like, for dinner?"

"I don't know. I doubt your mom wants to come home and cook."

"We could do it."

Pierce, eyes on the road, arched his brows and glanced at Declan.

"What?"

"Fix something, I mean. Like we could do breakfast for dinner and have it ready for Mom."

Pierce stared at Declan for a moment and finally nodded.

"Yeah. Yeah, that's a great idea, Dec. I think she would like that."

"Andrew says I should show her more respect. That it's a two-way street. If I want her to respect me…"

Pierce clenched his teeth and nodded. "Yeah. That's pretty wise, I'd say."

"I hated it," Declan whispered.

"Your therapy appointment?" Pierce wanted to yell, but he reminded himself to remain calm.

"No." Dec shook his head. "I hated it when my dad would hit her or push her around."

Pierce wasn't sure how to respond, so he waited to see if Declan said more.

"I hated when they fought, but I was so relieved the first time…"

"The first time what?"

Declan swung his gaze around to look at Pierce.

"She fought back."

thirty-five

. . .

WYNONA

She had come home exhausted, worried about what she would find to fix Declan for dinner. There were leftovers, and she had decided they would do, but she suspected Dec would growl about it.

What she didn't expect was to smell bacon frying when she opened the back door. Pierce and Declan worked in the kitchen; both of them wore aprons, the ones she normally wore. They didn't notice her at first, because there was music blaring. Something country, which surprised her. What was more of a surprise was seeing Declan singing along.

She stood for a moment in the doorway and watched the two of them move and work around each other as if they had done so a hundred times before. Declan was working the waffle iron. He grabbed plates from the cabinet while he waited. Pierce was flipping the bacon. The egg carton sat open on the counter, and when Pierce plucked each strip of bacon off the skillet and put it on a serving platter, he reached for the eggs next.

"Wow." She cleared her throat. She loved everything about her kitchen right now. It smelled delicious. She hadn't been sure she would be hungry after eating the lasagna earlier, but now that she was here, her stomach was growling again. She loved Pierce in his soft, worn denim and flannel shirt. The pink apron was a bonus.

But mostly, she loved the smile, the sheer contentment on Declan's face.

"A girl could get used to this," she announced.

Pierce peeked at her over his shoulder and aimed that smile at her. The one that did things to her. They still hadn't really addressed the night in her car. There had been some heavy kissing and petting since then, but Wynona still hadn't seen the body under the clothes he wore so well. She was ready. And she thought he might be, too. But they had been so careful about Declan.

"Hey, Mom." Declan grinned as the waffle iron beeped.

"Sit down," Pierce told her. "Everything's about ready."

Rather than argue—her kitchen wasn't big enough for it anyway—she slipped through the small room and dropped to sit at the table. Pierce cracked and fried five eggs. Declan plated the last of the waffles and carried them to the table.

"Do you want juice?" he asked her.

"Please," she answered with a nod.

She wondered how Pierce had talked him into this. But she wouldn't ask until later.

When they were all seated at the table, the breakfast spread in front of them, Pierce turned his phone down so the music was almost inaudible.

"How was the distillery, Dec?"

"So cool!" he gushed. "Have you been there, Mom?"

"I've had lunch at the Skeleton Bar."

"No, man. You should go to the distillery. Do a tour of all of it. It's just neat. The whole process. It's chemistry, Mom."

She nodded and glanced at Pierce.

"And what about the buildings? The—"

"Rickhouses," Declan supplied the word before she could say it. "Way cool. The old ones are really neat. But a lot of distilleries utilize them in different ways. Like, some don't rotate barrels, but others do. It affects the way they age, so it can change the color and flavor profile."

Wynona simply blinked at her son.

"They have this fungus on them, too. So freakin' cool. Like they look haunted."

She glanced at Pierce, but he only nodded.

"And what did you think of the bourbon?" she finally asked Declan.

He flinched and shook his head. "Not ready for that."

"Good." She and Pierce said at the same time.

"I'm glad I got to try it, though," Declan admitted. "That was way cool."

"Sounds like a good day."

"Thanks, Pierce." Declan glanced at Pierce. "It was fun."

"It was a fun day," Pierce agreed.

"Have you seen the amphitheater, Mom?"

"I have."

"That's gonna be cool, too. Branch said they anticipate it'll really bring in tons of people. So it should be a really good thing for the distillery."

"I think it'll be fun to see a concert there," Wynona decided.

"Yeah, me too." Declan shoved a huge bite of waffle in his mouth.

She glanced at Pierce again. He looked as contented as Declan. Wynona breathed a sigh of relief. Maybe things would turn around eventually, and Declan would settle in and find the right group of kids to run with. Maybe he would excel in school and find a good college.

When he finished the last waffle, he took his plate to the kitchen and loaded it in the dishwasher.

"I need to study," he told her.

"Okay."

"Thanks again, Pierce."

"You're welcome." Pierce watched over his shoulder as Declan vanished to his room. "You need to thank him."

"For what?"

"This." Pierce waved his hand over the table. "It was his idea to have food ready for you."

"Wow."

"I'm a little disappointed in the apron selection, though," he said with a frown. He picked up the apron Declan had left hung over the back of his chair. It was plain black. The one Pierce wore was plain pink.

"You couldn't arm wrestle him for the black one?" she asked with a smirk.

"The color's fine. I was hoping you had one that said *Kiss the Cook*. I'd have wrestled him for that one for sure."

"You want me to kiss you?" she quirked her eyebrows. "Is that what you're saying?"

"It is."

Wynona climbed to her feet and reached for him. Pierce tossed Dec's apron down again and followed her to the other side of the kitchen.

"Do you think we should talk about the thing?"

"What thing?" he asked as he settled his hands on her waist.

"About the night I took advantage of you in my car?"

He laughed softly and leaned closer to brush his lips over her forehead.

"I think we should do the thing again." He pressed a kiss to her cheek and nuzzled her neck.

"Me, too."

"Really?" He drew back to look at her. "Like, you wanna do the whole thing? Take our clothes off and take our time?"

"Mmm." She licked her lips. "I do."

"Well, we need to plan a night together, Wynona Herzog. Make sure Declan has something to do, and we'll get down to business."

"Thank you."

"For?"

"Taking him to the distillery."

"Honestly, Wy, it was fun. He's a good kid."

"He is, most of the time."

"No, he's a good kid who's made some bad decisions. Not unlike a million other kids out there. He was very courteous today with Branch. And very attentive."

Wynona smiled.

"Careful."

"What?"

"You're making me feel things, Pierce."

"Good." He pressed his lips to hers. "I plan to make you feel everything, Wy. All over your body, including what's in here and here."

He kissed her forehead again, resting his hand on her chest.

thirty-six

. . .

PIERCE

Lyndi greeted them from the living room when Pierce pushed the front door open. The smell of pumpkin pie hung in the air, though Pierce detected the smell of turkey roasting.

"Hey!" Lyndi put her iPad down and hopped off the sofa to meet them in the foyer of his parents' house. Dressed in leggings and an oversized sweater, she looked young and sweet—far too much of both to have been with Mav Pressey.

"Hi, Lyndi," Wynona returned the greeting as Lyndi gave her a quick hug.

"And you must be Declan." Lyndi brushed her fingers over the kid's upper arm, as if she knew a hug would be pushing it with him. "Declan, I'm Lyndi. Pierce's sister."

"It's nice to meet you," Declan said with a quick nod.

Pierce aimed a startled look toward Wynona when Lyndi threw her arms around him in a quick enthusiastic hug. Wynona only grinned as she unzipped her coat.

"Lyndi? Are they here?"

"We're here, Mom." Pierce shrugged out of his coat, surprised again when Lyndi took it from him and then turned expectantly to Wy and Declan. He turned toward the kitchen to greet his mom as Lyndi took Wy and Declan's coats and carried them to the hall closet to hang them up.

"Glad you're here." His mom hugged him hard and patted his back. Pierce returned her hug as fiercely, happy to be with his family, happy to be introducing Wynona and Declan to his parents.

"Mom." Arm around her shoulders, he turned her so she was facing them. "I want you to meet Wynona Herzog and her son, Declan. This is my mom, Gail Rooney."

"Wynona." His mom stepped forward, hand outstretched. Pierce held his breath for a moment, hoping his mom didn't say anything weird that would embarrass him. "It's very nice to meet you." The women shook hands, and then his mom immediately turned her attention to Declan. "And you, too, Declan."

"Thank you so much for having us," Wynona said with a warm smile.

"Any friend of Pierce's is always welcome," his mom said firmly. "Now, dinner will be ready very soon. But." She narrowed her eyes at Declan. "You look like a guy who could really use a homemade chocolate chip cookie."

Declan grinned and shrugged. "I wouldn't say no."

Wynona laughed softly and glanced at Pierce as Declan followed his mom into the kitchen.

"You okay?" He reached for her hand.

"Yeah, I'm good."

Fingers entwined, they followed Declan into the kitchen where Pierce's dad was leaning over the roaster, lid in his hand, checking on the turkey.

"Pierce." His dad didn't look up. "I need a beer, and you do, too."

Chuckling, Pierce moved away from Wynona to retrieve a couple of beers from the refrigerator. His mom busied herself with getting Declan not one but two cookies, and Lyndi appeared again, mumbling about mimosas.

"Dad." Pierce handed a bottle to him. "I'd like you to meet Wynona Herzog. This is her son, Declan."

His dad grumbled something unintelligible about turkey, gently replaced the lid on the roaster, and set the meat fork on the counter. He brushed his hands off, snatched his beer, and offered Wynona his hand.

"Hi Wynona, I'm Chuck."

"Nice to meet you, Chuck," Wynona said with a big smile. His dad nodded at Declan when he saw him eating a cookie.

"Gail makes the best cookies in the southern United States."

"Whatever, Chuck." His mom rolled his eyes.

Lyndi squeezed in by the island and handed a flute nearly filled with champagne to Wynona.

"We have orange, cranberry, or pineapple juice," she announced as she handed the other glass to Mom.

"Oh." Wynona arched her eyebrows. "Pineapple sounds delicious, but please let me get it."

Pierce watched Wynona ease into his mom's kitchen and rituals with ease. She sipped her mimosa as she talked with Lyndi and offered to mash the potatoes while his mom finished the gravy. His mom had rested her hand on Declan's shoulder early on, guiding him around the stove and the counter, showing him what was for dinner. Either that or threatening him that Santa would not come next month if he didn't eat his veggies. She had done that to Pierce and Lyndi when they were younger.

Pierce leaned on the counter by his dad, but he continued to watch Wy and Declan, and his dad's head was turned toward the living area. A Christmas movie was playing; Pierce glanced that way and saw the telltale sign—a smalltown community Christmas festival. They were probably singing "We Wish You a Merry Christmas." Lyndi must have had the movie on.

Wynona fit right in with his mom and sister, and he loved it. And Pierce wasn't sure it was possible, but it was almost better to see Declan at home in his parents' house, the easy grin on his face proof that he was enjoying himself. That Pierce's mom's teasing—if that's what she was doing—didn't bother him.

When dinner was ready, they served themselves and gathered around the dining room table. Pierce wasn't sure if it was by design or accidental, but Declan ended up seated between him and Wynona. He held his breath for a moment, wondering if that would upset Dec, but the kid seemed completely relaxed. His plate was piled high with all his mom's sides, even the dressing. Conversation flowed freely, and the laughter was quick and easy.

Declan stood to help dry dishes when Pierce's mom began washing them. Wynona looked at Pierce, obviously surprised. Proof to Pierce that Declan was a good kid, that Wy didn't need to worry she had ruined him. Pierce didn't know a lot about kids, probably less about teens—as far as parenting them. But he had been a teenage boy once, so maybe he had something to offer Declan and Wynona in that capacity.

Lyndi and Wy talked shopping, and Pierce and his dad retired to the living room to watch football. Pierce knew the kitchen was clean when Declan joined them, half a cookie stuffed in his mouth, the other half in his hand, ready to be gobbled up.

Later, after several games of Uno followed by Rummy, Pierce drove Wynona and Declan home. He wanted to go inside with them, but he knew if he did, he wouldn't want to leave. And that was dangerous.

The night Wy had straddled him in her car and ridden him to his release and he suspected, not hers, kind of felt like a dream. Sure, there had been some nice make out sessions since then. But Pierce wanted to be with her. He wanted to undress her, to cherish the look of her body and the feel of her warm skin pressed to his. He ached to lay her down and kiss her; her sweetness would rival any holiday dessert he would ever taste. And yet, he wouldn't push her. Not with Declan in the house.

"Coming in for a while?" Wynona asked him when he pulled into her drive.

"Mmm." He sighed and met her eyes across the front of the truck. Declan, sprawled over the backseat of the truck cab, cleared his throat.

"Um. It's cool," he mumbled. "You know. If you…"

Pierce watched him in the rearview mirror when he shrugged. His Adam's apple bobbed when he swallowed, clearly uncomfortable.

"Wanna stay." He finished, eyes locked with Pierce's in the mirror. "I mean. I'll, like, be in my room."

Before Pierce could react, Declan moved like a flash. He was out the door and halfway up the drive to the back door by the time Pierce turned his attention to Wynona.

"That was…" He frowned and shook his head. "Kind of…uncomfortable."

"Like when your girlfriend's dad eyes you suspiciously at the breakfast table early in the morning."

They shared a laugh. Wynona reached across the console for his hand.

"Did you have boyfriends over for early breakfasts, Wy?" He tipped his head. "Or did you sneak one into your bedroom at night?"

"I plead the fifth," she answered, leaning in when he moved to kiss her.

"You have no idea how badly I want to come in right now."

She rested her forehead on his cheek. "I do."

"And stay."

"I do," she repeated.

"I'd argue that you weren't loud the first time—"

"Only time."

He chuckled. "Only time we did it, but then, you didn't enjoy it."

Wynona tipped her head back and stroked her fingers down his cheek.

"I did enjoy it," she whispered.

"Not enough."

"Enough to want you again."

"I just don't want to do anything to screw things up with Declan." Pierce brushed a kiss over her forehead. "He's been doing so well."

"Well." She leaned back and arched an eyebrow seductively. "We could just do it out here. In your truck."

"I'd rather be curled up in your bed with you."

"Naked."

"So naked." He nodded.

"We could shut and lock my door."

"Let's go." Pierce shifted on the seat, his dick on high alert, ready to quit talking and get down to business.

thirty-seven

. . .

PIERCE

"We could wait," he said once they were inside.

Wynona, in the process of shrugging her coat off just inside the kitchen, looked at him in disbelief.

"I mean, just for an hour or something." Pierce shrugged.

"He's fifteen and no school tomorrow. He could be up until four in the morning."

"Still," Pierce hedged. "I don't want it to seem…like he gave us his approval, and we rushed in like kids to do it."

Wynona walked further into the kitchen and tossed her coat over the back of a chair.

"What?" Pierce unzipped his, but he froze when he felt her watching him.

"Thank you."

"For what?"

"I don't know." She shrugged. "Understanding? Caring about Dec?"

"Look." He stepped closer to her, coat open, and cupped her face in his hands. "I want you, Wy. But I want all of you. Your heart. Your soul. And I know that means Declan, too. I'm willing to do whatever it takes to have you both in my life."

Her smile was timid, her eyes glassy.

"Maybe you think it's too soon for me to feel this way." She swallowed hard. "But it's been so long since I've been this happy. This content."

Pierce pressed a soft kiss over her mouth.

"I'm falling for you, Wy." Pierce slipped his arms around her and pulled her close against him.

"Yeah?"

"Yeah." He grinned. "Maybe I love you."

"Hmm. Maybe I love you, too." She laughed softly.

"Let's just watch a movie. For a while."

"How about some popcorn?" she suggested as they backed away from each other. Pierce took his coat off and laid it over hers.

"After everything I ate tonight, you think I have room for popcorn?"

"Mm-hmm." She nodded.

"I do." He laughed and shrugged. "Sounds good. Want to holler at Dec and see if he wants to join us?"

Wynona stilled her hands as she reached for the pantry door.

"Never mind." She shook her head.

"What?"

"I do love you."

Pierce had been surprised when Declan had agreed to watch a movie with them. The three of them watched a couple of Christmas movies; he and Declan blew through two big bowls of popcorn, and Dec fell asleep in the recliner as the second movie ended. Wynona coaxed him awake so he could move upstairs to his bedroom where he would surely be more comfortable. Pierce cleaned up the small mess they had made.

Once Wynona turned the lights off and locked up, Pierce followed her to her bedroom, thrilled to have her to himself. In the glow of her bedside lamp, he undressed her slowly, reveling in each bit of skin he revealed. Kissing her. Tasting her. When she was nude, she pushed his hands away and began the process of undressing him. Pierce had been so busy fantasizing about having his hands on her, he hadn't considered how good it would feel for her to smooth her hands over his chest. To trace her fingers low over his belly and cup his cock. She wrapped her fingers around him, but Pierce moved quickly to distract her. The gentle press of his fingers between her legs made her swoon against him, and he was happy to lay her down on her bed and spread her legs.

She was quiet, though the soft, sweet and sometimes desperate mewling and purring told him she very much enjoyed the things he did to her body. And when they made love, he was sure to tend to her pleasure first, before giving into this own release. When both of them had surrendered and come back to themselves, Pierce simply kissed her. Short, sweet kisses. Long, tender kisses. And when she finally curled up at his side with her head on his chest, he lifted his head from the pillow to smooth her hair down and kiss the top of her head.

IN THE MORNING, PIERCE AWOKE TO THE PRESS OF HER FRONT to his back, her arm slung around his hips. He didn't want to move, to spoil the moment, but he knew Wynona had plans to shop with the girls today. They would all meet up later at 214 for dinner.

He linked his fingers with hers, a smile touching his face when he felt her soft kiss on his shoulder.

"I didn't want to wake you."

"Again."

"Again," she agreed with a soft laugh. She had woken him at some point in the night. Pierce had no idea what time it was when he felt her nibbling on his neck and then his collar bone. He had sprawled out on his back, allowing her to move over him, kissing his chest, his stomach as she did.

"You can wake me anytime, Wy." He twisted a bit to look at her over his shoulder. "Although, I have no complaints about sleeping with you in my arms, either."

"Technically, you're in my arms now."

He pushed gently until she moved enough for him to flop on his back.

"I am." He grinned. "I like that, too."

"Me, too." She kissed his cheek. "Want breakfast?"

"What time are you meeting the girls?"

"Nine. At Summer and Taj's house."

"What time is it?" he asked around a yawn.

"Seven."

"You don't have to make me breakfast."

"Maybe I want to." She winked at him as she tossed the sheet and comforter off to climb out of bed.

"Maybe I'd rather stay right here and enjoy the show."

She cocked her hip for him and then laughed as she snatched her panties from the floor.

"I do a mean strip tease," she said with a grin.

"Oh, I'll bet you do, and I wanna see it."

He watched her dress, not moving until she had zipped her jeans up and pulled a sweatshirt on and smoothed it over her hips. When the show was obviously over, he finally climbed from bed and dressed quickly.

"What's wrong?" he asked when he noticed her pouty face.

"I didn't get to ogle you dressing like you did me."

"Mmm." Pierce moved around the end of the bed to take her in his arms. "Want me to start over?"

They shared a long kiss, but she finally flattened her hand on his chest and took a step back. "Maybe you owe me one."

"I'm good for it," he promised.

He offered to help her make the bed, but she insisted he didn't need to worry about it, because she would throw the sheets in the wash before she showered. Instead, she grabbed her phone, stood on her tiptoes to kiss him again, and turned away from him. Pierce followed her to the door, but as she reached for the doorknob her phone buzzed.

"Probably Bristol."

"See? You're late. You don't need to fix breakfast."

"Not late." She shook her head as she pulled her door open, eyes on her phone. "Dammit."

"What's wrong?"

"Zach." She groaned as she led him to the kitchen. Pierce was stunned to see Declan in the kitchen, a stack of pancakes on a plate on the counter.

"What about him?" Pierce asked, dragging his gaze from Declan back to Wynona.

"You're up early," Wy said to Declan.

"Thought you might be hungry." He shrugged.

Wy glanced at Pierce, probably wondering what to make of Declan's comment.

"Thank you." She nodded.

"What about Dad?" Dec raised his eyebrows.

"He wants you to come and visit him over Christmas break."

Declan sighed and scratched his head.

"No." He put the plate of pancakes on the table, found the syrup in the cabinet, and grabbed the butter from the refrigerator.

"Dec. He's your dad."

Wynona sat down at the table and looked around. Pierce figured she was looking for coffee, but she wouldn't say so. She wouldn't want Declan to feel like he had forgotten something.

"I don't care, Mom." Declan stared at Wynona for a moment with a severe frown. "I don't wanna see him."

Pierce eased into the chair across the table from her, feeling like a third wheel in the conversation. He wanted to suggest to Wynona that if Declan didn't want to see Zach, she shouldn't force the issue. Not after that little talk he and Dec had had the other day.

But being the new boyfriend, Pierce kept his mouth shut. It wasn't his place to voice an opinion.

"Let's talk about it later, Declan," she suggested.

"When?" He pushed. "You're going shopping today and then you have that dinner tonight."

Wynona reached for a pancake.

"And I'm saying at Tyler's tonight. Remember?"

"I do remember. We can talk about it tomorrow," she said calmly. "There's plenty of time."

"Whatever," he grumbled as he stormed out of the kitchen.

"Dec!" Wy hollered after him. "Aren't you gonna eat?"

Declan yelled something unintelligible back at her. When Wynona started to stand, Pierce reached across the table and touched her hand.

"Maybe give him a minute," he suggested. "He talked a big game last night, but maybe he didn't like seeing us together this morning."

thirty-eight

. . .

WYNONA

Summer's SUV was loaded with bags. Wynona and her friends were all loaded from lunch, a few drinks, and a couple of shared desserts after said lunch. There had been easy conversation all day, topics ranging from Christmas memories, to shared steamy details, to worry over kids or parents. Wynona had never felt so at home with a group of women, at least not since her grade school years. And that didn't count. Who had a lot of memories, steamy stories, or worries over kids or parents in grade school? No, it was special to her to have these women as new friends, confidants.

They had all hooted and hollered when she admitted Pierce had spent the night with her. Bristol had mumbled as an aside that it was good Gail and Lyndi hadn't joined them due to volunteering at the Kissing Springs community center for the day. Being that Marlowe and Bristol, especially, were good friends with Pierce, Wynona was a bit stingy on the details she shared, but she said enough to blush while she talked.

Sheridan confided that she and Trey wanted a baby, but so far, they'd had no luck. Bristol seemed to take the news personally, which had confused Wynona. Until Bristol realized she was new enough she didn't know the entire backstory. So they had talked about Bristol's miscarriage and the fact that Trey hadn't even been around enough to know that she was pregnant, let alone that she had miscarried. The fact that he was now married to Sheridan, Bristol and Summer's sister-in-law, still blew Wynona's mind.

Marlowe told them her long distance guy—she had said his name was Cass—wanted her to go away with him for Christmas this year. Apparently, they had seen each other a couple of times since last Christmas when Cass had been in the Iron Stag with his buddies for someone's bachelor party. Marlowe was torn, because she wanted to see him. But she didn't want to leave Way over Christmas break.

Which had brought the conversation around to Declan. Bristol informed Wynona that Evan Church was recovering, healing well from the broken nose Dec had given him. Wynona had joked that hopefully Amy and Tony Church didn't hate her. Wynona also told them her ex-husband had demanded that Declan come and see him over winter break and that Declan didn't want to go.

Bristol and Sheridan insisted Wynona listen to Declan and not send him. Marlowe and Summer felt differently. While neither of them had a lot of good things to say about Zach, Marlowe had a son who didn't know his father. And Summer had seen firsthand the way divorce could hurt kids because of Taj's daughters with his ex-wife.

By the time they got back to Kissing Springs, Wynona was exhausted. Not really hungry, but anxious to get home and change for dinner at 214. She was ready for a cocktail and a night out with friends. And Pierce.

She had talked to Dec earlier on the phone. He had been running errands and hanging out with Pierce. Wynona knew he had been upset with her earlier, when she had suggested they talk about visiting his dad later. So it made her feel good knowing Declan was having a good day with Pierce. She knew they had been back to the distillery, though Pierce told her he wouldn't give Dec anymore whiskey to taste. She trusted him, but she doubted Declan would be interested anyway. While he had talked about the day at the distillery with Branch Lockland and Pierce often, rather enthusiastically, he hadn't been too keen on the bourbon itself.

Pierce was going to drop Declan off at Tyler Gordon's house on his way back to his place to get ready for dinner. Wynona took advantage of the quiet at her house for a long, hot shower. She turned on Christmas music while she chose her outfit for the evening—a short black cocktail dress she had purchased a while back and never worn because she and Zach had stopped going out and enjoying each other's company—and put her makeup on. When she was finished, when she had zipped her feet into her heeled, long black boots, she added a spray of perfume, a tiny pearl necklace her mother had given her when she was sixteen, and checked her look in the mirror in her bedroom.

She felt pretty.

But then, Pierce made her feel pretty in her mom jeans and old sweatshirts.

Still, it was fun dressing up. Dressing for an adult night out. Maybe they would go to the Boot Scoot to dance, and maybe she was dressed too fancy for that. But she didn't care. Pierce would be undressing her later, and she thrilled at the thought of watching his expression as he did so.

Feeling his hands, his mouth glide over her. The pressure of his length inside her. His sexy voice telling her he loved her.

She hadn't dared to dream that she would find love again, certainly not when she had driven to Kentucky on a whim, desperate to put distance between her current life and her past. But Pierce Rooney had given her everything she could ever want.

When he rang her doorbell, she turned the Christmas music off and answered it. Dressed in black trousers and a red button-down shirt, he looked like a Christmas present. One she was tempted to yank inside and open. And kiss. Maybe devour.

But when he whistled and leaned in to kiss her, she turned her head slightly so that his lips brushed her cheek.

"What's up?" he asked with a frown.

"I want a night out. I want dinner and drinks with friends. I want to dance with you. I want adult conversation. I want to laugh at dirty jokes and fun stories. And then I want you to bring me home and make me come so hard, I forget what year it is."

"I'm in." He nodded.

"If you kiss me now, we'll never get out of here."

"Well, you deserve that night out," he said with a smile, "so let's get to it."

"Thank you." She followed him outside and turned back to make sure the door was locked behind her. "How was your day?"

"Good." He grinned as he pressed his hand to the small of her back and led her to his truck. He pulled the door open for her and helped her up to sit. "We went to Lockland. Walked through a coupla rickhouses again. Talked about ricks. How they rotate barrels and why. He remembered pretty much everything Branch taught him that day."

"Good."

"We had pizza in Rodey."

"Sure he hated that," she said with a laugh.

"And we watched a movie at my house."

"I'm not even gonna ask."

"Indiana Jones," he answered. "He likes Harrison Ford."

"I do, too."

Pierce laughed softly. "I think you need to listen to him, Wy. When he says he doesn't want to go to Zach's."

She jerked her gaze from the windshield to meet his eyes.

"Okay."

"I know it's tough. As much as you needed to get away from Zach, he's still Dec's dad. And you're trying to salvage that." Pierce shrugged. "I get that. I respect that. But. You need to talk, and you need to listen."

"He talks to you." She frowned. "Doesn't he?"

"Not much, not really." Pierce shook his head. "But this is his first Christmas out of the house, the family unit, as broken as it was. Maybe it would be better to keep him with you, to keep him surrounded with the friends and family he's got here than to send him back to the house he used to live in."

Wynona smiled and looked away.

"I'm sorry." Pierce spoke quietly. "I don't want to overstep—"

"Family he's got here," she whispered and shook her head. "I like that. He does have family here."

"You both do," Pierce promised her.

thirty-nine

. . .

PIERCE

Wynona was beautiful in her dress. Hell, one look at her earlier when she answered her door, and Pierce had been ready to walk inside and lay her down. But he liked that she had stopped him, that she had told him she wanted a night out. That she wanted a nice dinner and drinks and time with adult friends. Didn't sound like she and her ex had done that often, not even before things got bad. So, Pierce was determined to give her a wonderful night.

He linked her arm through his as they walked into 214. His father had taught him to be a gentleman, so it was second nature to hold the door for her, to take her long wool coat and hang it up for her. But he was a red-blooded American male, so it was also totally normal for him to eye her long, lean legs and imagine what she might have on under her dress.

Knowing he would find out later, that they had her house to themselves and could make all the noise they wanted, put his dick at full salute as he escorted her to their table. Bristol and

Rhett and Sheridan and Trey were already seated. Pierce hoped like hell walking close to Wynona shielded his predicament until they took their seats. Wynona asked for a Kentucky Mule, so he ordered two when the waiter came around.

He talked with Rhett, Trey, and Taj when he and Summer came in. But all the while, he kept part of his attention on Wynona. How could he sit so close to her and not look at her? Tonight, for now at least, his favorite thing about her was her smile. The look of joy, of belonging, on her face was a far cry from that first time he had met her.

Part of him felt a little guilty for bringing it up about Declan and Zach. He hadn't wanted to ruin their night, hadn't wanted to elbow his way in somewhere that wasn't his business. And yet, he hadn't wanted to let the opportunity to talk to her about it slip by. Declan was finally settling in and finding a place for himself. Maybe she would have listened to Dec anyway, tomorrow, and together, maybe they would have decided the same thing. But it was important enough to Pierce to share his feelings. Thankfully, she hadn't seemed to mind; she didn't seem upset now.

Marlowe wandered into the place last with Mav Pressey. Pierce nearly choked on his drink, but Marlowe had thrown her head back and laughed.

"Nope." She shook her head at Pierce. "Just the date for the night. No dancing. No kissing. No anything else."

Summer snorted.

"How's it feel to be someone else's flavor of the day?" Taj asked Mav. Everyone around the table laughed. Since they were in no hurry, Marlowe and Mav ordered drinks before anyone decided on an appetizer or dinner itself. The swanky restaurant was packed as usual. Pierce knew they did good business; Tyler Jackson was a hell of a chef. But with this being a holiday weekend, every place in town was probably packed.

Instrumental Christmas music piped from tastefully hidden speakers. Pierce swept his gaze around the dining area, taking in the elegant holiday décor and the muted, ambient lighting. He'd long since quit grumbling about how fast restaurants and retailers switched into the Christmas mood. Why not just relax and join them?

Especially now that he had Wynona. And Declan. This Christmas would be extra special—his parents might be heading south after the holidays, his sister had come home, and the love of his life had appeared out of nowhere.

His phone buzzed in his pocket as the waiter delivered Marlowe and Mav's drinks. Wynona glanced at him as he slipped the phone out and glanced at it. He had feared it would be one of his parents, though thinking about emergencies with them was out of character for him.

The number on the screen sent a jolt of energy through him.

"Rooney."

Every head at the table swiveled to look at him. The Fire Chief's low, grumbly voice sent dread barreling through him.

"All hands on deck."

Pierce sighed and nodded. "Got it." He reached over and squeezed Wynona's hand as he pushed his chair back to stand. "Location?"

"Lockland Distilling."

"Say again." He froze at the table, heart in his throat.

"Lockland, Rooney. Getcher ass moving."

"Lockland," he repeated. "On my way."

He shoved his phone back in his pocket and looked around the table, finally meeting Summer's eyes. Wynona sat back and watched him with a look of concern.

"There's a fire at the distillery, Summer."

forty

. . .

WYNONA

Pierce dropped a quick kiss on her head. He was gone before she could blink. Wynona swallowed her worry, fear, and looked across the table at Summer. The distillery was her family's business. Her friend was pale, her hands shaking as she looked at her phone.

"Oh, God." She covered her mouth with her free hand, as if she might be ill. Taj rubbed her back.

"Let's go."

"You can't just go to the scene of a fire," Trey argued.

"It's her family business," Taj reminded him.

"I need to get to Mom and Dad." Summer's voice broke. "God, what if one of them—? What if the guys—"

"Summer." Taj took her phone calmly and hooked her chin in his fingers to make her look at him. "Hon, it's Black Friday. No one is at the distillery. Okay? No one is going to be hurt in the fire."

She swallowed hard and nodded, though she didn't look convinced.

"C'mon. Let's go to your parents' house." Taj stood and then helped her scoot her chair back.

"Taj, they have the kids," she sobbed.

"Okay." He remained calm. "All the more reason to go there. Don't panic. Maybe it's a small thing and already under control."

Wynona swept her gaze around the table. No one here believed that, but no one would say that out loud.

"Want me to come?" Bristol asked Summer.

"No. No. You guys stay and…" Summer shook her head as she stood. "Enjoy dinner."

Bristol swiped at her eyes as Summer and Taj hurried away from the table.

"Enjoy dinner," she mumbled. "How the hell do we do that now?"

"We say a prayer that Taj is right," Rhett said quietly. "That it's small enough they get it under control quickly."

"Hard part about dating a first responder," Marlowe said, eyes on Wynona. "The worry can make you sick."

Wynona nodded. "This is the first time I've seen him have to run out like that. It's a little nerve racking."

"He'll be fine," Trey insisted. "They'll all be fine."

"Remember the fire at Black Star Distillery? What was that? Like fifteen years ago?" Mav sat back in his seat.

"Was it bad?" Wynona asked when no one said anything.

Marlowe cleared her throat and nodded. "It was. Probably not a good time to go down memory lane, Mav."

Wynona took a deep breath and tried to relax.

"Has he ever been hurt? On the job?"

"A couple of minor things," Bristol said quietly. "Nothing serious."

"If a distillery is on fire, wouldn't the whole thing go up in flames? I mean…all that flammable—"

"Lockland has a huge water spray system with open nozzles as well as sprinklers. They're highly conscious of safety, including fire and the spread of fire." Bristol sounded like she was reciting from a manual. "Not to mention, our newer rickhouses aren't made of wood. Summer and her brothers are pushing to move to—"

"Most of them are made of wood," Wynona mumbled. Bristol knew that; maybe she was trying to make herself or Wynona feel better. "Declan talks about them all the time."

Mav explained to the waiter when he returned to take their order that a few of them had to duck out due to an emergency. The rest of them ordered dinner, though Wynona didn't think any of them would eat a bite. No sense in rushing home to pace the floors, and while she wanted to go to the distillery, she couldn't. No one should rush out there and get in the way. So why not order dinner and stay together?

Wynona wasn't sure if she was more worried about Pierce or the fire and the damage it would do to Summer's family's livelihood. If the fire raged out of control, there would be more chance for Pierce to be hurt, she knew that. The only time she had seen him at a fire was the night at that old garage. She didn't know a damned thing about firefighting, but it seemed to her that the guys working had been calm, confident. She also knew that Pierce took it to heart when someone was hurt or someone died under his watch. What would it do to him if there was excessive damage to Lockland?

The guys talked about football, and Wynona wanted to applaud them for it. They were trying to keep things normal, keep everyone's minds off what was going on just minutes away in Rodey. Sheridan picked at her scallops when their food arrived. Bristol simply pushed her plate away without touching a fork. And Wynona played with her wild rice for a moment before asking the waiter to box it up. Knowing it was ridiculous, that it was far too soon to know anything, she checked her phone several times, praying, wishing for a text or missed call from Pierce.

She needed him home, in her arms. No matter how much destruction the fire caused, Wynona would be there for Pierce. He had offered her his family, his friends, his heart. So she would love him through this.

forty-one

. . .

PIERCE

The flames had raged just over an hour after he arrived on scene. It crossed his mind that maybe he shouldn't be involved in this one, because he had a personal connection to the place. But the chief had directed all hands on deck, and the urgency of the situation had drilled him between the eyes when he arrived and saw the amphitheater burning. All that hard work, the money and time invested, just up in flames and gone in an instant.

He and Bowman had run the engine with the water pump, so he hadn't been that close to the flames. Still, the genuine possibility of any brother-in-arms being injured was enough to keep Pierce, keep all of them, in knots. The charred ruins of the amphitheater hunkered down in the darkness, the smell of smoke in the air, made him queasy.

Thankfully, the amphitheater was on the opposite side of the property as the rickhouses. But the fire could have jumped buildings and taken either the Skeleton Bar or the main visitors' center with it. The damage to the amphitheater was bad enough; at least the Locklands wouldn't have to close and shut down business for cleanup and reconstruction.

"Hell of a thing," Bowman grumbled as Gustavson and French pulled their masks off. Bowman and Pierce busied themselves reeling in the hoses buried in the Lockland property.

"It wasn't random," French announced. "Not like the place was struck by lightning."

"No faulty wiring," Gustavson agreed.

"Fuck, no." Bowman growled. "That was arson. You fuckin' know it."

"The same two who did the garage fire in Rodey last month?" Gustavson mumbled absently, clearly thinking out loud.

Pierce swayed on his feet.

"You okay, man?" Bowman glanced at him. "You inhale some smoke?"

Pierce shook his head and wandered away from the guys.

Arson.

Interesting timing. The day after he and Wynona spend the night together, the Lockland Amphitheater, yet to be officially named, went up in flames. A place Pierce and Declan had visited just earlier that day.

He leaned over to vomit, but his stomach was empty. There hadn't been time for dinner. The thought brought to mind Wynona sitting at the table at 214, watching him go, worry in her eyes.

Wynona and him laughing together as they walked out of her bedroom to find Declan, her son, watching them from the kitchen. Declan announcing that he didn't want to visit his father. Declan telling Pierce he hated Zach for what he had done to Wynona.

What if Declan had set the fire? For whatever reason. Because he was pissed that Pierce had slept with his mom? Because he had been planning it from day one? From the first time he had toured the distillery and learned about the lucrative business, the money, involved in the bourbon industry? Or maybe because he was afraid Wynona would force him to visit Zach? Maybe he was simply acting out because he felt like he wasn't heard. Maybe he *had* started the garage fire that eventually sparked the flame between Pierce and Wynona. Maybe the thrill of watching the fire catch, the flames leap and dance, had enticed him to do it again.

Or maybe *this*, maybe being arrested for arson, was his surefire way to avoid visiting his dad. It would be hard for Wynona and Zach to force him to visit if he was in juvie for this.

There had been no injuries, no loss of life. And yet, the amount of damage done to the amphitheater construction was staggering. Insurance might cover it, but that would most certainly drive up the Lockland premium.

Insurance wouldn't go an inch as far as mending broken hearts, though. And Pierce knew the Lockland family well enough to know this would break them. Healing would take some time. Hell, he wasn't actually part of the family, but watching those flames rage closer and closer to the Skeleton Bar and the visitors' center had left him breathless.

He cleared his throat a few times, spit out a mouthful of bile, and rubbed his burning gut and chest as he returned to the engine.

"Coulda been worse," Bowman reminded him.

"Could've." He nodded his agreement, desperate to get away from the scene. From the husk of the building he had just walked through with Declan earlier this afternoon. The hell of it was, he had no idea where to go. Part of him wanted to go to Wynona and put his head on her shoulder and maybe even cry.

And part of him wanted to find Declan Herzog and shake the shit out of the kid. What the hell had he been thinking? What if one of Summer's brothers had been in that building for some reason? A lot of business owners didn't take the holidays off, and Pierce knew for a fact that the brothers were often out here at odd times.

"He could've killed someone," he mumbled.

Bowman nodded as if in agreement. Any fire could kill someone. He hadn't read Pierce's mind. Right now, Pierce was the only person who suspected his girlfriend's son had set the fire. Never mind how he got from Tyler's house to the campus. It lined up, and Pierce's mind was made up.

Declan Herzog was responsible for a major fire.

The question was *how the hell did he handle it? Soft pedal it to the kid?* He didn't want Declan in juvie or prison, if he were arrested and tried as an adult. And yet, he couldn't turn his back on this.

Talk to Wynona? That would be the end of their relationship.

Then again, if he suspected Declan and said so, it would be the end of what they had only just started. And if he suspected, kept it quiet, and was proven right, it still would be the end of what they had only just started.

forty-two

• • •

WY

Wynona paced the floor, even after Rhett had brought her a cup of hot tea to calm her nerves. They had all left 214 together, but no one wanted to go home and be alone. Still, Wynona figured Bristol and Rhett might regret inviting them all to their house. For one thing, Wynona was bound to wear a path in the carpet as she moved mindlessly back and forth through the living room.

She was worried about Pierce. Of course, his friends here were worried about him, too. And yes, Wynona hated the thought of Lockland Distilling on fire, just as much as the rest of them did. But she and Pierce had only begun what she hoped was a long, happy relationship. What if she lost him now?

It would always be this way. She knew that. Pierce was a first responder, so anytime he was called out, there was risk involved. At least she knew Declan was safe at his friend's house. Often, anxiety about one thing bled into another and another until she was in knots and ready to shatter. That anxiety had led to a lot of fights with Zach.

She gave herself a mental shake. No need to think about him now, about his demands to see Declan. About Dec not wanting to visit his dad. She sipped the tea, now tepid, and glanced at the front window. The blinds were closed, but she knew even if she were to open them and press her face to the glass and look outside, she would only see darkness.

The room went still when someone's cell phone rang. Bristol glanced at Rhett in askance as he grabbed his phone from where it lay on the end table.

"Taj," he told them as he put the phone to his ear. Wynona wished he had put it on speaker phone, but since he hadn't, she watched his face closely as he spoke. He found her across the room as he listened and with a calm face nodded to her. She let out a deep sigh of relief, but in the next breath, her worry moved from Pierce to the Locklands, to the family business and legacy. Rhett nodded as he listened, eyes moving from Wynona to Bristol—another nod—and finally, he mumbled something that sounded like *thanks for checking in*. The room was so thick and still with tension when he put the phone down, no one moved or said a word. Every eye was on Rhett, though, waiting for the update.

"Pierce is fine," he said first. Wynona nodded, appreciating the sighs of relief she heard from the rest of the gang as Rhett continued. "No one was hurt." He glanced at Bristol and arched his eyebrows. "It was the amphitheater."

"Oh, no." Bristol flinched. Shoulders sagging, she dropped to sit on the edge of the sofa. "Oh, man."

Rhett sat beside her and smoothed his hand down her back. Wynona looked away, still overcome with relief that Pierce was okay, that no one was hurt. And yet, Pierce had given her the full tour and then some of the new construction out behind the Lockland visitors' center and the Skeleton Bar. She knew how much blood, sweat, and tears had gone into the project, not to mention the time and money. The Locklands already had acts booked for the following spring, and now, if the damage was bad enough, they would have to reschedule. Insurance would cover the rebuilding, but in the end, they wouldn't recover the prospected income for the following year. Not if there was extensive damage.

Thank God, the fire hadn't been close to the rickhouses. As bad as it was, a fire near the rickhouses would probably destroy the entire facility. Even with the firebreaks, the pond, and their buried hoses for just such occasions, distillery fires were dangerous and volatile.

"We're gonna head home," Trey announced. "Bristol, call us if you need anything, okay?"

Wynona saw Bristol lift her head just enough to nod at her ex, soon to be her brother-in-law. Sheridan leaned down to give Rhett and Bristol a quick group hug, waved at Wynona, and led Trey to the door. When they slipped out and the door clicked closed softly behind them, silence filled the room again.

"We're gonna go, too," Marlowe decided. Mav, leaning in the hallway door frame, straightened and jammed his hands in the pockets of his coat.

"Wynona, do you want a ride home?"

She wasn't sure she wanted to go home alone, and yet, she couldn't just hang out at Bristol and Rhett's all night, either. Surely, Pierce would call her when he could, if he didn't make it to her house tonight.

"Yes." She nodded and carried her teacup to the kitchen where she put it in the sink. "Thank you."

"Call." Marlowe dropped her hand on Bristol's shoulder and squeezed gently. "If you need anything."

"Thank you." Rhett, still sitting close to Bristol, nodded.

Wynona snatched her coat from the back of the sofa and followed Marlowe and Mav outside.

"You okay?" Marlowe asked as they walked down the driveway to Mav's truck.

"Yeah. I'm fine." Wynona cleared her throat. "Just a little nerve racking."

"It is."

"Thank God, they got to it when they did," Mav mumbled. He pulled the door open for the girls and headed around to the driver's side. "My dad knew the Kepner family. The Black Star fire was devastating."

Wynona hunched her shoulders and clenched her teeth together on the ride to her house. She was cold, but the trembling she felt now was a delayed fear response. Used to happen to her now and then with Zach, though less so as she grew more confident in her ability to fight back.

"He'll call," Marlowe told her when Mav slowed his truck in front of her house fifteen minutes later. Wynona flashed the two of them an uneasy smile and opened the door.

"Want Marlowe to walk you in?" Mav asked her. Wynona had the crazy thought that Pierce would be happy to know Mav hadn't offered to do it himself.

"No, thanks. I'm fine." She slipped out of the truck

awkwardly, thinking of Pierce's strong, but gentle hands helping her in and out of his truck earlier in the evening.

"Talk tomorrow."

Wynona nodded at Marlowe, closed the door, and pretended she didn't feel their eyes on her as she made her way to the door to let herself in. Exhaustion riddled her body, and her bones ached, as she undressed and washed her face. The roller coaster of emotions tonight had dragged her up and down too many highs and lows. She was ready for sleep.

But when she crawled into bed, she lay awake, staring at her phone, waiting for Pierce to call.

forty-three

• • •

PIERCE

He should have called her by now. When he left the scene of the fire, Pierce had gone straight home for a long, hot shower. Too worked up to sleep—the adrenaline rush had passed, but the nagging thoughts about Declan had him wound too tight to rest—he had dressed and paced his living room for a while. He texted her, a quick line to say he was fine and would call her soon. Pierce wanted to talk to her. He *had* to talk to her. No matter what would come of it, he had to see Wynona face to face so they could talk. Communication and honesty were far too important to him to put it off. He wouldn't just ghost her; even if he *wasn't in love* with her, Pierce Rooney wasn't the guy to let miscommunications or the silent treatment damage any relationship.

And yet, he had no idea what the hell to say to her.

When the numbers on the clock in his kitchen read 3:42, he gave up, locked his house up, and drove to her house. But once there, he only parked in the driveway and sat behind the steering wheel. The arson investigator would be on the scene at daylight. Pierce didn't know what he would find, but he sure as hell believed it would lead them right to Declan Herzog.

As a firefighter, as a member of the Rodey, Kentucky community, as an employee at Lockland Distilling, it was his responsibility to say something. Wasn't it? On the other hand, until there was hard evidence pointing to Declan, wasn't it best to support the woman he loved and her son? Her troubled son who needed help. Not judgment.

He knocked on the back door just before five, still uncertain about his intentions. Would he wake her? What if she was resting peacefully? How unfair of him to drag her out of bed and drop this at her feet. And yet, again, better to dig into the ugly honesty that would likely destroy them than put it off.

When she opened the door only seconds later, it was obvious she hadn't been resting peacefully. She had torn down her party look from last night, of course. The dress and heels had been replaced with fleece pajamas and fuzzy slippers. The makeup was gone; her eyes were puffy, as if she hadn't slept at all.

"Can I come in?" he asked quietly when she only stared at him.

She simply nodded for him to step inside. His body slumped with relief when she didn't verbally attack him for not calling. Once inside her small kitchen, he watched her close the door and then move absent-mindedly through the motions of making coffee. Only when she stood still in front of the counter, back to him, did he reach for her. Wynona turned immediately and pressed herself into him. Pierce wrapped his arms around her and drew her in close.

"Are you okay?" She dug her fingers into his back and held on.

"Yes."

"What's going on?" Tipping her chin up, she arched her brows at him.

Her words ripped into him sharper than her nails. With a slight flinch, he loosened his hold on her and closed his eyes.

"Pierce?" she coaxed in a gentle but concerned tone.

Of course she would know something was up, that he was keeping something from her. With a deep sigh of exhaustion and frustration, he dropped his hands to his sides and stepped back. Wynona shivered and wrapped her arms around herself.

"It was the amphitheater," he told her.

She nodded. "Taj called Rhett." She cleared her throat. "He said no one was hurt."

"No." Pierce shook his head. "No injuries. But the damage to the construction is bad."

Wynona winced, but she kept her gaze glued to his face.

"And?"

Dreading the words he knew he needed to say—he couldn't pretend about his worry over Declan and the fire didn't exist—Pierce scrubbed his hands over his head and finally covered his face.

"Wy."

"It was arson." She phrased it as a statement, not a question. But Pierce nodded.

"Yeah. The investigator will be on scene at daylight."

"Same people who started the garage fire?"

"I don't know." He shrugged.

Wynona was watching him when he finally rubbed his eyes and dropped his hands back to his sides. Their eyes met; the words Pierce didn't want to say on the tip of his tongue.

"You think it was Declan." Her voice was flat, void of emotion. Had she considered the possibility? Hell, she might have. She might have tossed and turned all night, worried about Declan. Worried that he had started the fire as some sort of rebellion, the same as Pierce had.

Feeling like a dick for leaving her to grapple with those dark thoughts on her own, Pierce reached for her. He froze when she shook her head the slightest bit and turned her back to him.

"I'm sorry, Wy," he said softly. "But…"

"Why?" she whispered.

"Why what?"

"Why do you think it was him? Did you find something that put him there?"

"No," he admitted.

"But?" She looked at him over her shoulder.

Pierce groaned and shook his head. Since she hadn't kicked him out of her house yet, he unzipped his coat and shrugged out of it.

"We were there. Today." He tossed it at a kitchen chair, ignoring it when it fell to the floor.

"You and Declan."

He nodded.

"And that somehow means he started the fire."

"Wynona." Pierce sighed. "Babe, Lockland has never had a fire. Dec and I spent a lot of time walking around the construction today. Talking about the music shows the Locklands want to host. Some of the acts Knox and Summer have been in touch with, trying to book. We talked about the bourbon industry—how big it is. How much money is involved."

She sniffled as she turned to look at him.

"He was with Tyler Gordon," she reminded him, but her words had no bite.

"Maybe. I think we both know how easy it is to sneak out and do things we're not supposed to do."

"I just don't get why he would do something like this."

"Don't you?" he asked gently. "He was upset this morning. Remember? First of all, I shouldn't have spent the night here. No matter that he claimed he was okay with it, I shouldn't have stayed. Second, he was upset about Zach."

"And I brushed it off." She moved closer to the table, yanked a chair out, and dropped to sit. "Jesus."

"It's not your fault." He smoothed his hand over her hair and down her back.

"Isn't it? I was selfish. Wasn't thinking about anything or anyone but myself. Last night. And this morning."

"Don't do that." Pierce shook his head.

"What're you gonna do?" She jumped from her chair, brushing off his concern, and stared at him intensely. "What're you gonna do, Pierce?"

"I don't know."

“You wanna turn him in.”

“I don’t,” he argued as he moved around the table to sit down. Wynona stood for a moment and watched him, her face drawn in a severe frown.

“You’re a community man. A standup—”

“I love you, and the last thing I want to do is hurt you and or Declan.”

“But you have to,” she whispered as she sat down again.

“I don’t have any proof.”

“I don’t want you to keep quiet about this, only to end up angry about it later. I can’t deal with that kind of—”

“Don’t ever compare me to Zach.” He shook his head. “I am nothing at all like your ex-husband, Wynona. That’s why we’re talking about this now. I won’t let it fester.”

She swallowed hard but said nothing.

“He’s a juvenile—”

“With how many strikes against him?” She tipped her head.

“He’s been in trouble, but he’s never been charged with a felony.” Pierce shrugged, noting how Wynona tensed at the word. “Has he?”

“No.”

“He could get probation. Home supervision and electronic monitoring.”

“And even that will come back and hurt him, Pierce,” she said quietly.

She was right. Arson was a felony, and if he was found guilty, no matter his sentence, the charge could hurt him in his future.

"I know."

Tears streaked her face as she stared at him.

"You can't live with your suspicions, Pierce. I know you well enough to know that." Wynona shook her head. "Especially with the fire being at Lockland."

"Maybe I'm not willing to lose you over this." He arched his eyebrows.

Wynona sat back in her chair, as if she needed to put more distance between them.

"And I'm not willing to let you do this for me."

"Maybe he didn't do it. Maybe we're—"

Pierce stopped talking when the back door banged open. Both he and Wynona swung their gazes toward the door, surprised to see Declan trudge in. Still in the cast, he looked more like a bedraggled ten-year-old returning from a sleepover with messy bedhead and rerun clothing than a sophomore in high school.

The scowl on his face deepened when he saw the two of them at the table watching him.

"What're you doing home so early?"

Declan dropped his bag on the floor and ducked his head for a moment. When he spoke, his voice broke. Wynona was out of her seat before Pierce could make out what he was saying.

"...see him." He finished the last few words on a roar. The red face, the anger in his frown, the tears in his eyes and voice—all of it nearly brought Pierce to his knees.

"Dec." Wynona took a step closer to him, but the kid put his hands up to hold her back. Pierce swallowed hard when she settled for resting her hands on Declan's shoulders. "I didn't say you had to—"

"You'll make me!" he bellowed. "You'll make me go, because you think somehow the father-son bond can be salvaged! Because that's how it's supposed to be. Never mind that I hate him for what he did to you!"

Wynona stared at her son, apparently stunned by his outburst.

"I don't want you to hate your dad," she whispered.

"It's not about what you want," Declan snapped. "*You* wanted to stay with him. *You* stayed and let him beat on you. *You* decided to leave. *You* told me I was going, too. *You* chose the middle-of-fucking-nowhere, Kentucky!"

"Declan."

Pierce flinched. Should he say something? Try to calm Declan down? Let him rage? Was it his business? Not really. But then again, maybe it was. Because he was part of Wynona's life now, enough so that her fifteen-year-old son had made them breakfast this morning, while Pierce was in bed with her.

"*You* don't get to choose what kind of relationship I have with him!" Declan roared.

"Okay." She nodded.

"I finally feel like I'm fitting in here. I finally have friends. And then *you* make me feel like I'm in the way, and *you* want me out of here!"

"Declan, that's not fair." Pierce shot to his feet. "You know your mom only wants what's best for you."

"I started that fucking fire!" Declan turned his rage on Pierce. "I did it! Because if I'm locked up in juvie, I sure as fuck can't go home and see dear old Dad, can I?"

Wynona flinched and sagged backwards against the cabinet. "Dec."

"How'd you get out there?" Pierce asked, suddenly needing Declan to prove he had done it. That he wasn't just seizing a bad opportunity to get himself in trouble, a desperate attempt to steer clear of his father.

"Patrick Hoffman."

The name was a sucker punch to his gut.

"I thought you were at Tyler Gordon's," Wynona whispered.

"I was. I got bored. Patrick picked me up."

"And you set the fire?" Pierce tipped his head.

"It was Patrick's idea," he mumbled, the energy and rage suddenly spent. "I told him—I told him you were with my mom, and that I thought we were, like, cool. But it was just… It'd be easier for you if you didn't have to deal with me. Right?"

"No." Pierce shook his head. "Not at all right."

"Patrick suggested the fire. At the amphitheater. Since you work there. At Lockland." Declan slumped against the counter opposite Wynona. "So I did it. And then I panicked. And then it hit me that if I turned myself in, there would be no way you could make me go back to Sioux Falls."

"What'd you use to start the fire?" Pierce's gruff voice drew Wynona's attention.

"Gasoline. And Patrick's cigarette lighter."

Pierce and Wynona exchanged a look.

"Jesus," Declan grumbled. "Now what? You don't believe me?"

"I do." Pierce barely breathed the words. "I do believe you, Declan. And I'm so disappointed that you would do something so ugly to good people like the Locklands. You didn't just hurt me. You hurt them."

Declan looked away.

"And your mom."

"What happens now?" Declan asked, careful to avoid eye contact.

"I guess you turn yourself in." Pierce shrugged. "If that's what you want to do."

"I just did."

"Nope." Pierce shook his head. "You told your mom's boyfriend."

"And you'll take it to the…chief…or whatever." Declan finally looked at him and rolled his eyes. "Mr. Good Guy."

Pierce stared at Declan for a long moment and finally moved to sit down again. He shook his head slowly, shrugged, and finally groaned with frustration.

"No. I'm not doing anything with it. Either you turn yourself into the police. Or gamble and see if they figure out it was you. Whatever you do, you have to live with what you did."

Declan's Adam's apple bobbed when he swallowed.

"Were you going to make me go back to Dad?" He directed that question at Wynona.

"No." She pressed her lips together. "No. I would have talked to you. Tried to persuade you that it's the right thing to do. But I wouldn't make you."

"Will I go to prison?" he asked Pierce.

"You're a juvenile offender," Pierce answered, "so, it's doubtful. But you could end up on probation. Or electronic monitoring. Counseling."

"I go to counseling," Declan reminded him.

"Well, you'll keep going."

Declan sniffled and looked at Wynona.

"I'm sorry."

The anguish in his words, in his voice, made Pierce's stomach roil and pitch. Wynona simply moved closer to the kid and put her arms around him. Declan rested his head on her shoulder and sobbed out loud.

Pierce considered slipping out. Giving them a moment. But Wynona met his eyes over Declan's head and reached her hand out to him. Climbing to his feet, he took her hand in his and closed in to put his arms around both of them.

"I'm sorry," Declan sobbed again. Pierce knew this time he was talking to him. While he appreciated the apology, he intended to have Declan offer it directly to the Locklands.

"Everything's gonna be okay," he said firmly.

"You can't know that!" Declan argued.

"I can. And I do. Because the Locklands are good people." Pierce laid a hand on Declan's shoulder and gave it a squeeze. "This is gonna suck, kid. You've got a lot of work to do to earn anyone's forgiveness and trust. But the Locklands are good people."

"I don't want you to hurt my mom." Declan pushed at Pierce, so he stepped back and dropped his hands to his sides.

"If you don't know me well enough by now to know I'm not a man who would ever raise a fist to a woman—"

Declan shook his head to cut him off.

"Don't leave her." Declan's voice broke. "Because of me."

Wynona sniffled and wiped at her eyes.

"I'm not gonna leave either of you," Pierce said simply. "That's a promise."

epilogue

. . .

PIERCE

The kid hadn't groveled, but his apology to Harlan and Jolene Lockland, all the way down to each of the Lockland kids and the employees, was heartfelt and sincere. Pierce had almost swept him out of the visitors' center after he spoke with the family, but Wynona had insisted he talk to the employees, too. Harlan, always a fair man, hadn't said much. Pierce knew his anger, his grief, over the loss of the amphitheater, the investment, was still raw, and pushing Declan too hard at him with the apology might do more harm than good. Jolene, on the other hand, had immediately forgiven Declan.

If Pierce knew the Locklands, and he did, Jolene would tuck the kid under her wing and protect him from here on out. Declan would be working for the Locklands, doing all the grunt work, the hard labor, for nothing for a long time coming, in an attempt to make amends for what he had done. It wouldn't be long before Harlan warmed to him, too.

The Lockland brothers, however, were a different story. Pierce was fairly certain Branch and Cole would eventually let it go.

But Knox was different, and it would take Declan a very long time to win him over.

Pierce hadn't said much more to him about the fire, about arson, the danger of what he had done. He *had* reminded him that he could have hurt himself and Patrick Hoffman, and if there had been anyone on the property, that person could have been injured or worse. But he felt certain that his words from that first morning, when Declan had broken down in front of him and belligerently confessed to setting the fire, had stayed with the kid. Pierce *was* disappointed in him.

But with each day that he drove Declan to the distillery or even to the Lockland's home to do any odds-and-ends jobs they had for him, Pierce was impressed with the kid's integrity and sincerity. Maybe the fire had been the catalyst for Declan to knock off the troublemaking behavior and be more responsible.

Then again, Pierce knew that remained to be seen. It was possible the guilt, the remorse, could wear off and Declan might jump back into breaking rules and causing trouble. The difference the next time would be Pierce would be around. Pierce spent a lot of time with Declan, whether it was that drive to and from the Locklands' where he worked for restitution or helping with homework or throwing a football around on the weekends.

Maybe he had a soft spot for the kid because his own sister had felt so out of place during her teen years. Maybe Pierce had picked up more on her struggles with friends and her mental health than he thought. Or maybe he had a soft spot for Declan because he was in love with Wynona.

Maybe it was just that when Pierce looked past that angsty teenage sneer—and he didn't see it too often these days—maybe he saw the bright, adventurous kid Declan was. And being with Declan, being around for him, had become just as important to Pierce as being there for Wynona.

"What?" Wynona, head tilted down over her iPad, looked up at him through her lashes.

"What what?" Pierce asked innocently.

"Why are you looking at me like that?"

"I can't look at a pretty lady seated at my bar?"

Wynona straightened and looked around.

"Do you do that often? Look at pretty women here?"

The Skeleton Bar was hopping, partly because of the holiday season. But the community was turning out for the Locklands, supporting them to help ease the burden of the lost construction and time. How could Pierce want to live anywhere else when people here took such good care of their own?

"There's a few from time to time," he said with a shrug. "But I only have eyes for one."

"Yeah?"

"Mmm." He nodded.

"What time is it? Do you think Declan is done scrubbing that cooler out?"

"Don't do that."

"Don't do what?" Her turn to act innocent.

"I'm putting the moves on you, Wy. Don't bring up Declan."

"Yeah? You gonna throw me over the bar and—"

"Whoa! Whoa!" He threw his hands up and laughed. "I

mean, sure, I've fantasized about that, but probably a good way to lose my job."

"Probably," she agreed.

"So, there's going to be a wedding in July."

"I never said I would marry you."

"I haven't asked yet." He leaned over to rest his elbows on the bar. "And when I do, I will talk man to man with Declan first."

She opened her mouth, but before she could utter a word, he shook his head. Wynona had thanked him time and again for stepping back and forcing Declan to handle his confession, his apologies. For forgiving him.

For loving them.

Enough so that Pierce didn't want her thanks anymore. Just her love.

Their love.

"What if he says no?" she asked instead of repeating her gratitude.

"Then I guess we'll live together in sin," he answered simply.

Wynona threw her head back and laughed.

"That is the sexiest thing I've ever seen." Pierce clenched his teeth.

"Whose wedding?"

"My friend Rye Gallaher and his fiancée, Chantel."

"I haven't met them yet."

"You haven't. But you will."

"When?"

"When you are my date for their wedding."

"You're being a bit presumptuous."

"Well, being that we're sleeping together, I thought it was safe to assume you would go with me."

Wynona grinned and nodded. "Yes."

"Yes, you'll be my date, or yes, you'll marry me?"

"You haven't asked me yet," she reminded him.

***

Thank you for reading Pierce and Wynona's story! Please consider leaving a review on your favorite bookish site!

seducing you

Chapter 1

"Dibs on the guy in the cowboy hat."

"No kidding, Chan." Nova Brathwaite rolled her eyes. "The bet *was* a cowboy."

Chantele Morgan eyed the two guys bellied up to the bar. Both were dressed in jeans that displayed their assets nicely, both wore cowboy boots, but the guy on the right wore a worn-looking cowboy hat and the one on the left wore nothing on his dark hair.

"The other guy looks as much like a cowboy as the hat guy," she decided. She pounded the rest of her longneck and looked around the bar.

"So?"

Chantele looked at her other friend and arched her eyebrows. "What?"

"What's your plan?" Paisley Hathaway sipped from her club soda, put her glass down, and watched Chantele with a smirk.

Chantele had thought marriage had made her friend Paisley glow, but the baby she was carrying—never mind that it was roughly the size of a plum—brought out a shine in Paisley's eyes Chantele hadn't seen in twenty-seven years of friendship.

"What?" Chantele relaxed back in her chair and waved a hand over the silky tank and skimpy bra that barely covered her own assets. "This isn't enough?"

Across the table, Nova snorted. She finished her cocktail and looked around for their waitress. The Iron Stag was a mix of trendy and greasy spoon, and the result was bizarre, yet interesting. The three of them had come here mostly because it was the closest place to the VRBO house they'd rented for the weekend. There weren't a lot of bars or restaurants near Rodey, Kentucky; if they wanted a change of scenery later or tomorrow, they would have to pile in Paisley's SUV and head to Kissing Springs, Kentucky. The Bourbon Boot Scoot sounded like a fun bar. And they could always check out the male revue that performed at The Boyd Theater.

If Chantele struck out here with the cowboy at the bar.

Paisley grinned and shrugged. "Absolutely enough, but you gotta get him to turn his head this way before he sees 'em."

"True." She looked around again. "I was thinking some line dancing."

"Girl, you need a pole, not a line." Nova shot her a frown.

Chantele dropped her head back for a full-throttle laugh. She felt her cheeks heat with the suggestion, but the lighting in the bar was good for hiding things like blushes.

"She can shake her ass with the best of them," Paisley reminded Nova, who pointed at her with her glass still in hand.

"Well, how's this for starters." Chantele stood and reached for Nova's empty highball glass.

"What're you doing?" Nova cut loose with a rip of her contagious laughter.

Chantele winked at Nova. "Since our waitress is working so hard, I'm gonna go to the bar and get us another round. Pais? You need another club soda?"

"Nope," Paisley answered with a sigh. "I'm driving."

Chantele laughed softly and nudged her shoulder. "You wanted that little bun in your oven."

"Six more months." Paisley's fake groan didn't fool Chantele.

"Longer if you breastfeed," Chantele reminded her. "Just sayin'."

"Not sure she wanted the bun in her oven," Nova mumbled, "but she sure as hell likes the sausage that put it there."

"Jesus." Chantele rolled her eyes. "I'll be back, *ladies*."

The jukebox—apparently, the Iron Stag was behind the times as far as DJs and music machines, but they did have a live band playing *next* weekend—played "Maybe It Was Memphis" as she made her way up to the bar. Her cheeks tingled a bit knowing her friends were watching her, expecting her to say something to the cowboy.

She would, but she wasn't sure this was the right time. First, she just had to catch his eye. Get him to notice her. She could do that. That part wasn't a problem. But Chantele wasn't much for hookups. Unfortunately, that was the crux of the bet. Her friends—she'd been besties with Paisley since kindergarten and Nova had wandered into the fray in junior high—knew she wasn't a hookup kind of girl and had bet her she couldn't ride a cowboy before the weekend was over.

Never mind that they were here for Paisley. To get Paisley out for one more good time before the baby she carried was bigger, before she was exhausted, and maybe even dealing with morning sickness. The three of them had always gone all-in with dares and bets. Chantele supposed she'd started it back in tenth grade when she dared Nova to offer the varsity quarterback a blowjob. When she'd reported back after the party they'd all crashed, Chantele and Paisley had believed her without question. They'd seen Nova sneak off with him, and they'd seen him appear by the bonfire about fifteen minutes later with a big smile on his face.

Nova had taken her turn then and dared Paisley to sneak into the admin offices and hide Mrs. Carey's favorite coffee mug. Paisley had gone one step further, stolen the coffee mug, and left a ransom note in its place.

Since then, the dares and the bets—the money and favors exchanged had started later, after they'd started college—had only gotten wilder.

Chantele leaned her elbows on the copper bar and tipped her head back to study the wooden rack that hung over the whole area. Chopped up bourbon bottles hanging from wire housed old-fashioned light bulbs—the kind that put out too little light to be much more than interesting.

The prerequisite mirror Chantele had come to expect behind every back bar in America was absent. In its place was an impressive display of liquor bottles, the lion's share of them being bourbon.

Welcome to Kentucky.

She'd come to the Bardstown area once before with her ex-boyfriend. Their relationship hadn't fared well on the Bourbon Trail, but damned if she hadn't loved the experience and the bourbon. She could thank John for that, she supposed.

A pour of Elijah Craig barrel proof or Old Ezra sounded good, but Chantele wasn't sure switching from her trusty old friend light beer to good, high proof bourbon was a wise move. Not when she was supposed to be seducing a cowboy.

Then again, maybe a little shot of something stiff and high proof was just exactly what she needed. Paisley was here. She would make sure Chantele and Nova didn't get black out drunk.

"Whatcha need?"

The bartender was easily six feet tall, bare arms covered in tattoos. Distracted by the ink on the woman's hands, it took Chantele a moment to focus and order.

"Just a gin and tonic," she finally found her voice, "and another longneck."

"Got it." The woman reached, grabbed a longneck from a cooler behind the bar, and popped the top off all without looking. Chantele could whip up a marketing plan for this bar that would rock all of Kentucky, but she couldn't do *that.* Impressed, she mumbled a thank you and took a long pull of her beer.

She turned to peek at the cowboy. He'd looked good from her seat at the table thirty minutes ago when he'd first walked in with his friend. Up close like this, Chantele might need a bar napkin to wipe up her drool. His hair—what she could see of it under his hat—was a mix of honey blond and caramel. Shirt sleeves rolled up over his wrists put his tan, sinewy forearms on display. He had big hands; she blushed again just imagining what Nova would say about that. No rings. No watch. Just a leather cord around his right wrist.

When the guy with him noticed her looking, Chantele nearly died of embarrassment. She felt flames shooting out her cheeks, and her knees went wobbly—less of a swoon and more of an *oh, shit, I'm dead* feeling.

Own this, Chan. If you're gonna seduce a guy this hot, you gotta play the part.

"Howdy."

The greeting from the other guy, the realization that she was watching them, turned her cowboy's lips up in a small smirk. Chantele wasn't impressed with the howdy. She wanted to ride a cowboy, not settle into *Green Acres* and meet people who loved farm livin'.

Still. The smirk on her cowboy's face was delicious and worth it.

"Hey." She gave them a polite nod.

Nova would be all over the guy by now. Paisley would play hard to get. Chantele still didn't know where she stood with guys and her friends and her mode of operation. Or maybe she just didn't have a modus operandi. Or mojo. Or whatever it was that had hooked Paisley a hot, devoted husband, and snagged any hot guy in the area to warm Nova's bed on her whims.

"You're not from around here."

Still the other guy talking.

Chantele glanced at the bartender when the woman gently shoved Nova's drink at her over the bar.

"Thanks."

"Where you from, darlin'?"

The guy doing all the talking was hot, but she decided he'd be more attractive if he stopped talking.

"Lexington," she answered, because why not? She wanted his friend to say something, so engaging in conversation with the talker was probably her best route.

"City girl." The smooth talker nodded. Chantele took another drink of her beer and turned to them, resting her right elbow on the bar. She wasn't completely helpless around men, but damned if she knew what to say.

"Anything fun to do around here?" she asked, channeling Nova.

"You're looking at it, honey."

Unsure if the guy was referring to drinking and dancing at the Iron Stag or himself, Chantele only nodded and gave them both the eye. Nova Brathewaite had that whole side-eye, once over down to an art; Chantele hoped she'd learned a little something from watching her friend through the years.

Her cowboy's smirk had grown into a real smile. The scruff around his mouth, the mustache, and the way his longish hair curled around the collar of his shirt was such a turn-on, Chantele felt her nipples harden under her silk tank.

Great.

They're not going to miss that.

As expected, the smooth-talker's eyes took a ride over her shoulders and lit up when he noticed the THO. He probably thought she was into him.

"You here alone, City Girl?"

"No," Chantele answered the talker, but her eyes were locked with her cowboy's warm, cognac-colored gaze. "Here with some friends."

She took another pull from her beer, feeling a jolt of lightning zing her tight little nipples all over again when the cowboy dropped his gaze to peek at her.

"You guys have a good night." She flicked her eyes over to the guy doing all the talking, but she was quick to look back at the cowboy. His eyebrows jumped a bit in surprise, but he held the smile and his tongue, and Chantele made her way back to her friends. She made sure to put a little swing in her step, laughing with her friends when she plopped back down in her chair.

"How'd it go?"

"No idea," she answered. "But I could probably do the other one right there on the bar if I wanted to."

"Yeah?" Paisley leaned a bit toward her to look at him around Nova.

"Don't look!" Chantele shoved Paisley back gently.

"Careful, careful!" Paisley laughed. "The other guy was interested?"

"Yes, because I have a vagina."

"Pretty sure guys don't think of our kitties that way," Nova mumbled with a pensive frown. "You're not into him?"

"Nope." Chantele shook her head. "His ego's bigger than the state of Kentucky."

"Yeah, but I wonder how big his cock is."

Chantele choked on her beer and rolled her eyes at her friend. "I'm sure he'd show you."

"I'm pretty sure I'll ask." Nova shrugged.

"Well, just so you know," Paisley turned to Chantele with a frown, "Nova's hookups here don't get you out of the bet."

"Hookups?" Nova yelped. "Plural?"

"Just sayin'," Paisley answered with a grin.

Want to read Chantele and Rye's story? Click here:

Seducing You

also by tracy broemmer

Women's Fiction Novels:

Luther's Cross 10th Anniversary Edition

Just Like Them

Small Hours

Picket Fences

Two Story Home

Say Everything

Sketching Litchfield Lake

Damsel

The Valentine Suite

Fairytale

Green-Eyed Girl

Come Home For Christmas

Ever, Again

Safe as Houses

Every Little Thing, Lorelei Bluffs, Book 1

Two A.M., Lorelei Bluffs, Book 2

Blind, Lorelei Bluffs, Book 3

Leaving July, Lorelei Bluffs, Book 4

Hesitation Marks, Lorelei Bluffs, Book 5

Four Letter Words, Lorelei Bluffs, Book 6

See Kate, Lorelei Bluffs, Book 7

Loved You More, Lorelei Bluffs, Book 8

A Lorelei Ending, Lorelei Bluffs, Book 9

I Do, Lorelei Bluffs, Book 10

Truth Is, The Williams Legacy, Book 1

Other People's Ugly, The Williams Legacy, Book 2

Omissions, The Williams Legacy, Book 3

Contemporary Romance Novels:

Destiny's Calling: Your Future Is Waiting

Wedding Day Shenanigans

Holiday Fling

The Kiss Off

Something Like Love

Plus One

Hold Onto the Stars, Book #5 in Blue Collar Romance series

The Jane Thing, Book #2 in Meet Cute Book Club series

Doctor Divine, Doctors of Eastport General, Season 2

Beach Daze, Flamingo Island

Moonlight in Montreal, The Vagabond Series

Christmas and Other Inconveniences, Betting on Christmas Collection

A Naughty Lesson, Most Eligible Bachelors

Eggnog in Amesbury, Christmas in Amesbury Series (SWEET ROMANCE)

A December Wish, Wishing for Love Series (SWEET ROMANCE)

Shameless Santa, Kissing Springs Bourbon Fever Collection, Book 1

Sunshine & Soulmates, Kissing Springs Bourbon Fever Collection, Book 2

Bourbon & Bedposts, Kissing Springs Bourbon Fever Collection, Book 3

Midnight AND Mercy, Kissing Springs Bourbon Fever Collection, Book 4

Love, Nashville, The Mississippi Queen Trilogy, Book 1

Forever, Duncan, The Mississippi Queen Trilogy, Book 2

Always, Jess, The Mississippi Queen Trilogy, Book 3

Gettin' Hitched, The H Books, Book 1

Hookin' Up, The H Books, Book 2

Holdin' On, The H Books, Book 2.5

Intoxicate Me, 515 Whiskey, Book .5

Taste Me, 515 Whiskey, Book 1

Contemporary Romance Novellas:

Indian Summer

Dear Jaclyn Perris

French Stuff

End in Flames

Mistletoe Mishaps

Toasted: A New Year's Eve Novella

Boone's Girl

Trusting Cupid

Makin' Whoopsie!

Swipe for Fangs

Swipe for Ghouls

Feels on Wheels (Love in Motion Duet, Book 1)(SWEET ROMANCE)

Rings on Wings (Love in Motion Duet, Book 2) (SWEET ROMANCE)

Love in Motion Duet Boxset (SWEET ROMANCE)

Endless Summer (Timberton Hounds)

Homeless Holiday (Timberton Hounds)

Restless Hearts (Timberton Hounds)

The Timberton Hounds Novellas Boxset

Seducing You (Welcome to Kissing Springs: Bourbon Fever & Lockland Distilling: Keys to Love Trilogy)

Kissing You (Welcome to Kissing Springs: Bourbon Fever & Lockland Keys to Love Trilogy)

Other Novellas:

The Devy Man, A Horror Novella

Today, Again (Sweet Love Story)

Women's Fiction Short Stories:

India Falls

Luther's Cross: 87,600

The Candy Cane Tree of Willow Lane

Delays

Same Time Next Year

Contemporary Romance Short Stories:

Perfect Pictures, The Wine Tasting Series, Traminette (SWEET)

Coming Home, The Wine Tasting Series, Edelweiss (SWEET)

Save Me Every Dance, The Wine Tasting Series, Rosé (SWEET)

Marry Me, The Wine Tasting Series, Shiraz (SWEET)

Birthday Wishes, The Wine Tasting Series, Muscat (SWEET)

Dad Jeans, The Wine Tasting Series, Vignoles (SWEET))

The Wine Tasting Series Boxset (SWEET)

Peppermint Lane

Priceless Memory (Timberton Hounds)

Truly Dante, A Mississippi Queen Trilogy short story

Strawberry Wine

Love Letter

Leaving You, Welcome to Kissing Springs: Bourbon Fever & Lockland Distilling: Keys to Love short story

Sambuca Santa

Deadman's Hollow

about the author

Tracy is the author of several contemporary romance titles, including Plus One, Wedding Day Shenanigans, The Mississippi Queen Trilogy, and the H Books—Gettin' Hitched, Hookin' Up, and Holdin' On. Tracy also writes women's fiction and is the author of the Williams Legacy series as well as several stand-alone titles.

Tracy's books have been called gripping, emotional, and timely, and readers describe her characters as real and relatable.

Tracy lives in Midwestern Illinois with her husband of 31 years.

Find her on the web at www.broemmerbooks.com

www.ingramcontent.com/pod-product-compliance
Lightning Source LLC
LaVergne TN
LVHW091116080826
845145LV00008B/1932

* 9 7 8 1 9 6 5 3 3 1 1 6 3 *